***Someone was***

"I've got fresh flov̶[...] [...] [...]y [...]
favorite."

Trigger words. She dimly knew this, but
couldn't seem to pull herself out of the awful
place he'd sent her.

A woman screamed. Again. And again.

Lea hunched over, cradling her midsection,
as if by doing so she could stop the blows. She
knew exactly what Feiney was doing to that
woman. She'd been there, experienced it, up
close and personal.

Marc grabbed her, yanking her up close to him,
wrapping his arms around her while stroking
her hair. "You're safe," he muttered, over and
over. "Safe. Hear me, Lea?"

Dimly, she was able to focus enough to nod.

Then, he covered her mouth with his and
kissed her.

\*\*\*

Become a fan of Silhouette Romantic Suspense
books on Facebook and check us out at
www.eHarlequin.com!

Dear Reader,

This book, Lea's story, is devoted to the third of the Cordasic siblings. Being captured by a deranged serial killer would mess up anyone, but Lea is a trained and extremely competent FBI agent. Or she was…until The Cowtown Killer got a hold of her.

Now, struggling to pick up the pieces of her shattered life and regain a sense of competence and purpose, Lea is shocked to learn her abductor has escaped from prison. But rather than run and hide, she knows the only way to regain her life is to face him and beat him at his own game.

Marc Kenyon has long loved Lea from afar, but after his screwup led to her being captured, he believes the loathing he sees in her lovely eyes is directed at him. When he offers to help her capture their nemesis, he hopes they can both obtain redemption. And maybe, just maybe, his love will heal not only her, but himself.

I became very attached to this family and finishing this book was bittersweet. As you can see in the dedication, I cherished your letters and hope you enjoy reading Lea's story, *Profile for Seduction,* as much as I enjoyed writing it.

Karen Whiddon

# KAREN WHIDDON

*Profile for Seduction*

ROMANTIC
*SUSPENSE*

SILHOUETTE BOOKS

ISBN-13: 978-0-373-27699-8

PROFILE FOR SEDUCTION

Copyright © 2010 by Karen Whiddon

This edition published by arrangement with Harlequin Books S.A.

For questions and comments about the quality of this book please contact us at Customer_eCare@Harlequin.ca.

® and TM are trademarks of Harlequin Books S.A., used under license. Trademarks indicated with ® are registered in the United States Patent and Trademark Office, the Canadian Trade Marks Office and in other countries.

Visit Silhouette Books at www.eHarlequin.com

**Printed in U.S.A.**

## Books by Karen Whiddon

---

## KAREN WHIDDON

started weaving fanciful tales for her younger brothers at the age of eleven. Amidst the Catskill Mountains of New York, then the Rocky Mountains of Colorado, she fueled her imagination with the natural beauty of the rugged peaks and spun stories of love that captivated her family's attention.

Karen now lives in North Texas, where she shares her life with her very own hero of a husband and three doting dogs. Also an entrepreneur, she divides her time between the business she started and writing the contemporary romantic suspense and paranormal romances that readers enjoy. You can e-mail Karen at KWhiddon1@aol.com or write to her at P.O. Box 820807, Fort Worth, TX 76182. Fans of her writing can also check out her Web site, www.KarenWhiddon.com.

To all the readers who sent letters,
who wrote me because they were eagerly waiting
for each Cordasic story. Thank you!

# Chapter 1

"Just because he broke out of prison, doesn't mean I have to go into hiding," Lea Cordasic argued, the expression in her hazel eyes fluctuating between frustration, anger and pain.

"He broke out of maximum security by using a broom handle to slip under a five-thousand-volt electric fence, just like the St. Clair Springs, Alabama, case in 2001." Stan Clements, SAC and resident jerk, wagged his finger at her. "He told his cell mate he was coming after you. No way in hell am I letting you anywhere near this psycho."

"You're being ridiculous. You need my help to catch this guy."

Watching her, Marc Kenyon was struck by three things. One, how beautiful and passionate she was. Two, he felt horribly responsible for much of her pain. And three, judging from the impassive expressions of the other men in the room, she was fighting a losing battle.

"I'm sorry." Stan flashed her a fake smile. "But we can't allow you to—"

"Can't allow?" Lea's voice rose. "Do you have any idea what's at stake here? Once Feiney starts killing again—"

"You're too personally involved. You haven't even been certified to return to work, for Chrissake," Stan exploded. "Why are you even at the office? I don't understand what you're doing here."

Lea's beautiful eyes narrowed. "I came as soon as I heard about this. It's all over the news—Cowtown Killer escapes, on the loose. If you're trying to contain information, you're not doing a good job."

"That still doesn't explain why you're here. No one called you in."

"Oh for the love of…" She turned to Marc, the man closest to her, the only other person in the room besides her who didn't belong. The one sheriff in a roomful of FBI agents.

Knowing his feelings for her colored his judgment, he saw what she wanted in her gaze. Though she had no idea how he felt about her, she hoped he'd help her now. The connection they'd forged in one life-altering event still held for both of them. And on top of that, he owed her. No one knew that better than he did. Feiney would never have captured her if Marc Kenyon had been on his game.

"Kenyon, will you please tell this stupid SOB why I have more reason than anyone to want Feiney back in prison?"

"Don't even bother." Stan shot Marc a furious look before pinning his gaze back on Lea. "This is FBI business. He's here for the Feiney case, nothing else. I've read the file. I know what Feiney did to you. You're messed up, Cordasic. That's why you're on a medical leave of absence."

"I'm ready to return," she argued. "I know better than anyone how Feiney thinks, how he operates."

Stan continued as if Lea hadn't even spoken. "Medical leave, Lea. Even if you were able to return to work today, there's no way in hell I'd let you anywhere near this creep. Go home. Get some rest. We'll handle this case ourselves. Us and the Tarrant County Sheriff's Office." He inclined his head at Marc, the only one in the room who should have been in uniform, but wasn't. "Feiney will be back in his cell in Huntsville before you know it."

"But—"

"Go home, Lea." Stan pointed at the door. "Now. I've got a team to brief and a meeting to run."

Tossing back her long auburn hair, Lea lifted her chin and smiled. In that instant, Marc knew the gorgeous special agent didn't care what Stan said. She wanted Feiney, and if they wouldn't let her join the official hunt, she'd do it on her own. At this point, anything the Bureau or the sheriff's office said or did would only get in her way.

A moment later, she confirmed this. "You should be aware that I'm going after him." Her long-lashed gaze swept the room, including Marc in her scornful stare. "With or without your official sanction."

"Don't even go there." Stan sounded tired.

"I'm not asking your permission." Standing, she moved toward the exit.

"You know as well as anyone here we can't let it become personal. When you do, you make mistakes."

"Then I guess I'm going to make the biggest mistake yet."

As the door swung closed behind her, no one spoke. Lea Cordasic, decorated FBI agent, had just gone renegade. She meant to try and capture a monster on her own, without the FBI's sanction.

Worse, Marc Kenyon knew he would do whatever it took to help her, even if he had to go up against the Bureau himself. He owed her—and himself—that much.

Striding from the building to the parking garage, Lea vibrated with fury. Not only had the Bureau humiliated her to begin with by taking her off active duty, but now this. Denying her the only case that mattered to her. Personal, true. They were one hundred percent right about that.

But they all knew no one was better suited for this team. She, more than any of them, had the most at stake.

She hated who she'd become. She'd give anything to change back to her old self.

Before Feiney had captured her, she'd considered herself an invulnerable badass. Feiney had taught her fear, and she despised the bitter taste it left in her mouth. She'd do anything, absolutely anything, to get rid of it.

Catching Feiney herself would definitely go a long way to repairing the damage.

But the Bureau didn't want her help. Instead, adding insult to injury, they'd brought Marc Kenyon in on the team. Technically, his office was in charge of the investigation. But Marc? A lot of good he had done them before. It'd been on his watch that she'd gone undercover to catch a monster, and the monster had caught her instead.

She bit back a surge of rage as Feiney's deceptively genial face popped into her mind. Six months of therapy and she could finally think about him without shaking with rage, but the nightmares continued. Though her therapist had high hopes, Lea privately thought the dreams would cease only when Feiney was dead. She forced herself to picture him often, like someone who couldn't help testing a wound to see if it was getting better. So far, it hadn't healed.

And now, the SOB was back on the loose.

Instead of getting in her car, Lea reversed direction and hit the sidewalk. She needed to clear her head, so she began walking, working up to a slow jog. She didn't have on running shoes—too bad. On the plus side, she wasn't wearing heels, just a pair of simple leather flats. She pushed everything out of her mind except the rhythm of her stride, the easy cadence of her feet slapping the pavement.

Focusing again, Lea realized she'd gone several blocks from the office. Cloaked in sweat, she slowed. She moved her foot and winced. Blisters. Great. After her release this had happened often, losing herself in her running. Now, not so much. Until today. Now that Feiney was free again, before she could go on the hunt, she had to take precautions, to make sure everyone she cared about was protected.

First on the agenda—make sure her mother was secure. She had to get her mom out of town. That presented another set of problems. If Lillian Cordasic got even the slightest hint that Lea was trying to protect her, she'd dig in her heels and resist.

With gray hair cropped short in a practical cut and her shoulders slightly rounded from the weight of her years, she was the matriarch of the Cordasics. Not only had she lost her husband, who'd followed the family tradition of working in law-enforcement intelligence, but she had single-handedly raised three children who'd all grown up to do the same. She was the rock of the family, the nucleus around whom they all revolved.

Tied to the wall in Feiney's dungeon, Lea had cried for her mother. Lea's weakest moment and one she'd never forget.

Worse, Feiney had heard her and played on this,

threatening to go get her mother and make Lea watch him torture her. Lea could all but hear him in her head. Her worst fear right now was that he'd try to grab her mother and use her to reel in Lea, the only one of his victims who'd escaped. She had to make sure her mother stayed safe. The problem was, she couldn't go to her mother directly with her fears.

Lillian Cordasic didn't scare easily. And, since she was the only person on the face of the earth—other than Dr. Spender, Lea's psychologist—who even had an inkling of what Gerald Feiney had done to her daughter while he'd held her prisoner, she hated the man with a blazing passion that nearly rivaled Lea's. The more that Lea thought about it, learning the Cowtown Killer had escaped would more likely send Lillian to the shooting range for target practice than make her flee. Her mother was tough that way.

Therefore, the first call Lea made would be to her brother Dominic. She'd need him to come up with some reason for their mother to visit him and his wife Rachel in Vegas. It'd have to be something good, something that required Mom desperately. Otherwise, once Lillian learned Feiney had escaped, she'd never leave town.

"Sure," Dom agreed instantly, not questioning the brief scenario she outlined. "Even better, why don't you come out here with her?"

Lea suppressed a twinge of guilt. Her brother didn't know she'd been placed on a leave of absence. "I can't. I'm working the case."

A long silence fell, then Dom cleared his throat. "Are you sure that's wise?"

He knew her so well. Blinking back unwanted tears— damn Feiney—she had to struggle to keep her voice level and her tone even. "Dom, I caught him last time. Who better than me?"

"True," he soothed. "But he also put you through hell, and it's only been six months. Not long enough."

"Yes it is," she insisted.

"What does your shrink say?"

"I haven't discussed it with her," she said stiffly. "I'm not in the habit of checking my every decision with her."

"This time you should. This guy is a major nutcase." Another pause, then Dom snapped his fingers. "Hey, why don't I come down and help you out. Mom can visit here with Rachel and Cole. It's a win-win."

"She won't go if she thinks I'm in danger," Lea responded immediately. "You know how protective she is. Plus, I don't need your help, thank you. You don't work for the Bureau anymore, remember?"

"Yeah, I do remember. Right now, I'd say it's a good thing I don't. Your SAC is an idiot if he wants to put you through this again." He exhaled sharply. "Wasn't he even concerned about compromising evidence?"

Lea shook her head. That was the problem with telling lies. They started off simple and just got more and more convoluted. "I told him he had no reason to be."

Dom cursed. "You damn Feebs have no sense sometimes. Have you told Seb?" Their other brother, Sebastian was probably going to blow a gasket, too.

"I'm calling him next. And no doubt he'll subject me to the same crap."

Dom laughed. "It's only because we love you, baby sis. You know that."

"I do. So you'll call Mom and invite her up? I'll even pay for the plane ticket."

"No need." He laughed again. "Rachel will be glad to see her, too. I'll phone her right now."

Relieved, Lea hung up then punched in Seb's number. This time, she got voice mail. With a disgruntled sigh, she left a message. Her brother had recently married the love of his life, the popular country music superstar Jillie Everhart, and though back from his official honeymoon, he was so over the moon that the entire family teased him about enjoying an extended honeymoon.

With plans underway to make sure her mother would be protected, Lea could breathe a little easier. Glancing at her watch, she tried to decide how long she should wait to call her mom herself. She wanted to give Dominic time to do his stuff, and if she called too quickly, her astute mother would realize something was up—if she hadn't already. Since Feiney's escape was all over the news, it was only a matter of time. Dom would call her back once everything was settled.

Her cell phone chirped and she answered without even glancing at the face, figuring it was either Seb returning her call or Dom letting her know everything was set.

"Lea, my Lea. Oh, how I've missed you." The gravelly voice was instantly recognizable. A voice from her worst nightmares.

Shocked, she nearly dropped the phone. Steady. Steady. Deep breath.

*Feiney himself.* She should have been expecting this. After all, they were tied together more intimately than most lovers—a fact she not only despised, but wanted to remedy.

"How did you get this number?" She channeled her instinctive jolt of terror into fury, letting the clean, sharp knife of rage clear her head.

"I have people." He sounded smug. "People that take care of me, find me what I need. They know how important you are to me. We are meant to be together."

"I can't wait to see you." Choking out the words, she let

her hatred propel them. "When I do, you'll be back behind bars."

Though she should have been, she wasn't surprised when he laughed.

"I have no intention of going back to prison," he said.

"What the hell do you want?"

"You," he answered instantly. "You know that, Lea. Even while inside Huntsville, I've been following you over the past year, having reports delivered to me when I was locked up. I know everything about you, Lea Cordasic. Everything. After all, you belong to me."

Repulsed, for one heartbeat…two, she couldn't even speak. No. No. She would never allow him to silence her again. Never.

"I've been keeping an eye on you, too," she said. This, at least, was true.

Feiney gave a satisfied sigh. "Ah, you still underestimate me."

"Believe me, I never underestimate you." Nor would she ever again. Once was enough.

"Lea, I've missed you. Do you remember how good it was when we were together?"

Good? When she'd been his prisoner, chained in a dark, windowless room in a basement? Son of a…

"I do remember, Feiney. Very well. In fact, I can't wait to get back there—only this time, you'll be the one in chains. And I'll take care of you. Good care. You can count on that, Feiney."

She'd stunned him into silence. Hell, she'd even shocked herself. This part of her—dark and twisted—hadn't been there before he'd captured her. Maybe if she turned the tables, she could finally exorcise it.

The sooner the better.

Spinning on her heel, Lea sprinted back toward the

building. She needed to notify someone right now and get them to trace the call.

Evidently hearing the sound of her feet slapping the pavement, Feiney laughed. "Running? Why? You can't trace me. I'm at a public pay phone and, by the time you send people to get me, I'll be long gone."

He chuckled, the sound sending shivers down her spine. He'd laughed at her often in those endlessly bleak days six months ago. Laughed at her refusal to lose hope, her refusal to curl up in a ball and give up, like all the others had.

In the end, she'd had the last laugh. Sort of. A team had come for her. Marc Kenyon, from the Tarrant County Sheriff's Office, had led the charge. No doubt he'd thought that by doing so, he could make up for the screwup, *his* screwup, that had let Feiney get her in the first place.

For him, maybe it had worked. As for herself, she hated him. For his screwup, true, but more than that because he'd been the one to see her, weak, near death, naked and covered in filth. She'd been shocked when she'd read in his face how close she was to dying. Marc had freed her, wounding Feiney in the cross fire.

On the surface, she'd been grateful, Marc had been solicitous, and the Cowtown Killer had gone to prison. Case closed.

Only not for her and, she suspected, not for Marc either. Lea had gone to the hospital and Marc had dutifully visited her twice, common courtesy among coworkers. She'd choked out her thanks and he'd grudgingly accepted, or so it had seemed to her. He'd had trouble meeting her eyes or even looking at her and, God help her, she'd understood. After all, she'd been the worst failure of his career.

In the end, Marc had gone back to work, Lea went on medical leave and started therapy.

"Are you afraid yet, little Lea?"

She struggled to find an answer, something to say that wouldn't reveal either the depths of her horror or the fierceness of her determination to track him down and stop him.

"No," she lied. "I'm not afraid. And, for your information, I'm not running, I'm walking."

He laughed again. "I know you walk for recreation. I hope you'll be careful out there, all alone in the predawn hours. You never know who might be watching."

Trying to breathe normally, she slowed her pace. Warning her? He was actually warning her? Why? Feiney wasn't stupid. Still walking, she wiped her free hand on her slacks, trying to dry it. Now, more than any other time, she needed to be calm, cool and collected. Despite the fact that the mere sound of his voice sent her spiraling back to that dark time, when she'd been his prisoner and he'd held her life—and her sanity—in his twisted hands. Games. He was all about games.

Another call beeped in the background. Both of them ignored it.

"What do you want?" she asked again.

"We've covered that already. You. I want you."

"Why?" she asked, proud that she managed to keep her voice level.

He laughed again. "You're my love, the only one strong enough to match me. You're the only one who ever escaped," he told her. "My only piece of unfinished business. But more than that, you're special. My soul mate."

Gritting her teeth, she forced herself not to concentrate on the sheer blasphemy of his words. Rambling, he didn't even notice.

"Darling, I had to escape, so I could find you again. I'm not one to leave things undone. We were meant to be together. Forever and always."

He began humming. With a sense of revulsion, she realized he was humming the song he'd played over and over when she'd been his prisoner.

As a trigger, it worked. The horror of what he'd tried to do to her came rushing back, slamming into her like a sledgehammer to the skull. She nearly staggered, but instead straightened her shoulders and took a deep breath.

"I'll never concede." She spoke her thoughts out loud. "Even then, you wouldn't have been able to break me. Come and get me, Feiney. Let's find out."

There. She'd just issued a challenge. She had to be careful here. Egotistical maniac he might be, but the man's IQ had tested in the genius range. Though Feiney had just reiterated that she was the reason he'd escaped prison, he wouldn't be too eager to go back.

So she'd play the game. Carefully, adroitly, hoping in the end that she hadn't telegraphed her moves.

"Don't call me again," she rasped and pressed the end call button. Breathing hard and fast, she stared at her phone as though the electronic device had suddenly become possessed.

When it started ringing again, she declined the call. Shuddering, she couldn't seem to stop shaking with a hodgepodge of tormented emotions.

Through it all, she knew only one thing. Once a captive, she was now a huntress. Only that, nothing more, nothing less.

And that would have to be enough.

Oh, God. Wiping at her face, she realized with a numbed sense of shock that tears were silently streaming down her face. She wouldn't let anyone see her like this. Since her release from captivity, not even her mother had seen her cry.

Her therapist would expect a call so she could deal with the residual emotions. No. Hell no. Everything inside her recoiled at the thought. She wasn't up for that long, slow stare and the low-voiced question—always the same— *Hmm. How does that make you feel?* If she heard that again, she'd gag.

For some odd reason, her thoughts returned to the tall, handsome deputy. He'd rescued her, and she hated him for it, but she didn't really know him. Determinedly, she put him from her mind and set about getting back to normal.

Straightening her shoulders, she rolled her neck to work out any lingering kinks from the stress. She took a deep breath, knowing she'd need a minute to gather up her shredded composure and try to put herself back together. She'd worked through this once and believed she'd come to terms with it. Apparently not. She felt a flash of anger, furious because she sure hadn't expected to have to work though it again.

If anything, this strengthened her resolve, making her even more determined to be the one to bring in Feiney. And pray she had enough self-restraint not to kill the bastard.

"Hey! Lea. Wait up." Speak of the devil. Marc Kenyon, shouting her name.

Slowing, she blinked, swiping at her face again, hoping she didn't look too ravaged. Schooling her expression— game face on—she stopped and turned, waiting while he jogged up to her.

With a dispassionate eye, she evaluated his well-fitting dark suit—which looked expensive—and starched white shirt and red power-tie. He looked put together and professional, except for his unruly mane of blond, surfer-dude hair. With his classical profile and ever-present tan, he could have been the perfect representative of his home state, California. She suspected that hair was how he did so well undercover. The man didn't look like a cop. Didn't act like one either.

And she hated his guts.

"What do you want?" Not bothering with civility, she crossed her arms.

His ocean-blue gaze bored into her. "Are you okay?"

"What's it to you? The legendary Marc Kenyon." She edged her voice with a trace of mockery.

He ignored this. "I've been trying to call your cell. Stan gave me the number. After two tries and getting voice mail every time, I thought maybe…"

Though he didn't finish, she knew exactly what he meant. He'd thought Feiney had gotten her. No doubt he didn't want to be rescuing her again.

"No worries. I'm fine." Pulling out her phone, she switched it back on. "Sorry, I couldn't click over. And a minute ago, I turned it off. Now that that's established, you can go."

"I wanted to talk to you. I know it bothers you that Feiney's loose and you're not on the team," he said.

"Not exactly rocket science. So?"

"I know how you think," he began.

At his words, irritation flared. She had so much trouble keeping her emotions under control these days. "You know nothing about me," she snarled. "Let's keep it that way." Moving off, she had to restrain herself from swearing as he jogged to keep up.

"You're angry. I can understand that…"

"Can you?" she asked, her voice dripping with sarcasm. "I don't think so." *Angry* didn't begin to describe how she felt. Sometimes she thought fury would consume her. She—trained in martial arts, a competent markswoman and a freaking FBI agent, for God's sake—had allowed herself to be captured by a serial killer.

Everything she'd endured at Feiney's hands was almost secondary to that humbling fact. She sometimes felt as if she actually deserved what she'd gotten. This infuriated her even more, making her burn with her emotions, night after sleepless night.

More than everything, she wanted to kill Feiney. Two things stopped her—one, her deep respect for the law and her job as enforcer of that same law; two, the insidious knowledge that were she to give in to her baser desires and shoot the bastard, she would become him. Or, in her own way, as like him as she would ever become.

Therefore, she wouldn't shoot him. No. But she *would* capture him. She personally wanted to bring him in silently, under cover of darkness, without alerting the media, to bring him in cuffed and chained and then maybe right before she turned him over to the other authorities, she wanted to spit in his face.

Certainly, loathing guided her, that and a kind of awful certainty that if she wasn't the one who brought him in, she'd never repair the shattered threads of her self-confidence. Never banish the all-pervasive fear and anger for good.

This man, Marc Kenyon, had seen her at her lowest moment. For that reason alone, he couldn't know her.

"I know you hate me," he said quietly, surprising her. The bleak look he gave her reminded her of herself.

"You're not the only one who is personally involved in this case," he said, his tone biting. "You may not remember, but I was part of the team assigned as your backup when you went undercover back then."

"I remember," she said, impatient, not completely understanding.

"Do you?"

About to answer, she inhaled and nodded instead.

refusing to slow her pace. If he insisted on wasting her time talking to her, he could simply keep up.

"The day Feiney captured you, I was the one monitoring the van. I was the one listening in case you needed backup."

Again she nodded, still not understanding. "I know all this. What's your point?"

"When Feiney grabbed you, I didn't understand what was going on. If I'd acted sooner, I could have sent in backup. I could have *saved* you, gotten you out of there and maybe captured that bastard without you having to go through what you did."

At his words, she felt the oddest sensation. Like being adrift on an iceberg in an endless blizzard. A moment later, the feeling passed.

*This* was why he thought she was angry with him?

"Look, Kenyon." Now she did slow slightly, forcing herself to meet his gaze. "I don't blame you for that. How could you have known? There was no way anyone could have foreseen what happened that night."

"We were monitoring your wire. We had two undercover agents watching you. When you disappeared—"

"I went to the restroom," she said mildly. "No one could have known he would be waiting there for me with chloroform."

He shook his head, the raggedness in his voice telling her he didn't get it. "Even so, when you didn't return, I should have sent in the full team."

"In what? Five minutes?" She scoffed, deliberately making her voice hard. "Feiney knocked me out and had me out of there in less time than it takes to blink."

"We still don't know how he got you out of there. Since the restroom only had one tiny window, he must have arried you out in full view of our agents."

As gently as she could, she pointed out the obvious, even though she knew if he was anything like her, he must have gone over the facts in his head a hundred times already.

"The bar was crowded. The back door was right next to the restroom. It was simpler than it should have been."

Marc only shook his head, unwilling to let her absolve him so easily. "I failed you. I want a chance to make it up to you."

Jeez, this was the last thing she needed, especially right now.

"You rescued me. Imaginary debt repaid. Let it go, Kenyon."

"You should never have been there." He took a deep breath, his rugged features inscrutable. "I let you down."

"We've already been over this," she interrupted. "We were part of a team. Feiney was sneaky and smart and he did something we didn't expect."

The hard set of his jaw told her he wasn't listening. "My job was to protect you. We should have had a man stationed at the back door, near the ladies' room."

"Shoulda, coulda, woulda." It sort of amazed her that she could sound so blasé about this now, talking to him. "We all make mistakes. My mistake was not expecting Feiney to be in that restroom."

He stared at her, expression inscrutable. "How could you possibly expect that?"

She pounced on that. "Exactly. If I couldn't, how could you?"

"Surely you don't blame yourself?" Disbelief rang in his tone.

"Of course I do." The only other person she'd ever admitted this to was her shrink. "For a brief period of time, the bad guy won. My job was to keep that from happening."

"You honestly think—?"

"Apparently, so do you," she shot back. "Isn't that why we're both so driven to capture him ourselves, no matter what the cost?"

Silence, while he considered her words. Then he jerked his chin in a nod, telling her he got it. "I think you have a shot at getting Feiney. You understand him. I do, too—I've studied the case obsessively since he went to prison. I want to help you. I think if we work together as a team, we'll get the bastard."

# Chapter 2

This stopped her short. "Are you serious? I've been ordered to stay away from the investigation. There's no way the sheriff's office will condone this."

"I'll take that chance."

"Why? What's in it for you?"

He looked away and somehow she understood he was about to lie to her. Or, if not lie outright, omit part of the truth.

"I want to sleep at night."

"Do cops ever sleep at night?" she shot back. "I don't."

"Did you, before Feiney?"

"None of your business." She started running again. Marc Kenyon moved too close to her reality while attempting to evade it himself. Still, he made her damn uncomfortable. She kept remembering the look in his eyes when he'd found her. He'd believed her inches from death's door.

"Come on." Once again, he caught up with her, his easy stride telling her that he was no stranger to exercise. "We would make a good team."

"Pithy. And a load of bull. You want to work together and you won't even be straight with me." Slowing to her walk, she once again wished she was wearing her running shoes instead of flats. With the right shoes, she just knew she could leave him in the dust.

As if he could see her thoughts in her face, he pushed his hand through his hair. "You want truth? Fine. We need to work together because we're the same. Neither one of us has a chance at feeling normal again until we get Feiney back behind bars."

Damn. She opened her mouth and then closed it. What could she say to that? She knew he was right. Of course he was right.

That didn't mean she had to like it.

Still, as she looked at him, handsome and competent and unable to get past what he regarded as his greatest mistake, she felt a grudging sense of kinship.

Though her office and his worked together, she'd had little contact with him before the Feiney operation. Since then, she'd learned more than she'd wanted to about Marc Kenyon.

Others called him a rebel. Some said his rescue of her and subsequent capture of the Cowtown Killer had saved his career. She didn't know and certainly didn't care.

After all, she still saw his face in her nightmares. He'd been the first one in when they'd come to rescue her. Looking in his eyes, she'd seen a reflection of how close to death she was, how helpless, how weak.

She hated him for that.

Yet she was pragmatic. Had to be. Having a partner

and backup made perfect sense. But him? She would have preferred someone else. Anyone else.

But they weren't exactly lining up at her door to work with her, were they?

"Look, Kenyon—"

"Marc. Call me Marc." He stared at her, searching her face.

"Marc." She swallowed. "I'm gonna tell you the truth." Or part of it, she amended silently. "Every time I look at you, I see his face."

A muscle worked in his jaw. "Feiney's?"

"Yes."

"That's exactly why we need to work together to catch him."

Twisted logic, but curiously, it made sense.

"I don't know," she began.

"Why'd you turn off your phone?"

Should she trust him? Maybe this would be a good test.

"He, uh, called me. Feiney."

Marc swore. "We need to notify the team."

Brightening, she nodded. "Maybe then they'll let me join them. Hold on." Turning the cell back on, she punched in Stan's direct number from memory. The call went directly to voice mail.

"Stan's not taking my calls. It's kind of hard to give him any information if he won't talk to me."

"True. I'll call him later and explain. What'd Feiney have to say?"

Taking a deep breath, she continued. "He's back to his old games." Briskly, she repeated what her nemesis had said.

"That scumbag is going to pay," he ground out. Marc scanned the surrounding area.

"He's not here."

"Then why were you running?"

She shrugged. "Not because he was chasing me. I like to run. It helps to relieve tension."

Nodding, he appeared to take her statement at face value. All cops had some way to relieve stress. Some chose religion, others hobbies, many alcohol. Lea ran.

"What'd he want?"

She thought for a moment before answering. "Me. He claims to believe we're soul mates."

He watched her with narrowed eyes. "And?" he prodded.

As she was about to speak, her phone rang again. As she raised it to check the caller ID, Marc snatched it from her hand.

"Talk to me," he snarled, and then listened. A moment later, with a sheepish look on his handsome face, he handed the cell back to her. "This guy says he's your brother. His name is Dominic."

Unable to keep from grinning, she held the phone to her ear. "Hey, Dom. Did you talk to Mom?"

"No." Her brother's voice vibrated with barely concealed panic. "When was the last time you saw her?"

"Yesterday. Why?"

"She won't answer the phone. I left a message on the answering machine and then tried the cell."

"So? Maybe she's busy. I'm sure she'll call you back."

Dominic made a sound—part exasperation, part embarrassment. "Yeah. Maybe. But I got impatient. I texted her 811." Their own private, family code which meant *not an emergency, but still urgent. Call immediately.*

"And then?" Lea asked, both dreading his answer and knowing what he was going to say.

"And then nothing. She never called me back."

"I'm sure there are a thousand reasons," Lea said, managing to sound confident even though her insides had turned to ice. "No way Feiney got her."

Beside her, she sensed Marc Kenyon going tense. She ignored him.

"If he did…" Her brother swore.

Lea glanced at her watch. "He hasn't had enough time. It hasn't been more than a few minutes since I got off the phone with him."

"Got off the phone with him?"

Mentally, she groaned. "Yeah. He called me."

"How'd he get your number?"

"Probably off the Internet. He was really good at that kind of stuff before he went in. A professional hacker, remember? Anyway, my point is that he hasn't had enough time to call me and then grab Mom."

"Unless he called from her house," Dom said, sounding both pissed and worried.

Damn. She hadn't thought of that. Normally, in any other case, she would have. Why she hadn't this time, she didn't know. She couldn't afford any slipups, not with Feiney.

Fear stabbed her, sharp and sudden. "The house," she repeated. "I don't think so, but better safe than sorry. I'll go there right now and check on her."

"No." Dom sounded adamant. "Not you. Call the police or send some of those other Feebies you work with. You don't need to be anywhere near where Feiney might be."

"It's my case."

"I'll pull strings. Call your SAC."

"Don't you dare," she hissed. "This is my job, my life. I can take care of myself. I don't want you messing with my career, you hear me?"

"I hear you. But I can't help being concerned. I still think you should let someone else handle this one."

"Whatever. I'm gonna let you go now. I'll call you when I find Mom." Disconnecting the call, Lea glanced at Marc. "Sorry to run, but I've got to go check on my mother and make sure she's all right."

"Feiney?"

Reluctantly, she nodded. "It's a possibility. He's targeting me, therefore he'll target my family."

"I'll go with you." Marc's tone left no room for argument.

"That's not necessary," she said stiffly. "You heard what I told my brother. Ditto for you. You've got a job to do, a team to keep you briefed."

Slowly, he shook his head. "Are you always such a hard-ass?"

"Go away." She shooed him with her hand. "Good luck with the case, Kenyon. Nice seeing you again."

He didn't move. "Sorry. I'm going. You need backup. Especially if Feiney *is* there..."

The thought terrified her, making her throat close up, which brought another shot of rage that she had to tamp down.

No one—especially Marc—could know how danger-ously close to out of control Feiney made her feel.

Still... She glanced at Marc's broad shoulders and well-toned physique. No harm in taking along a little backup. She could hold herself together. After all, she'd been doing nothing but that for the last six months.

"Fine. Let's go." She spun around, heading back, trying to look confident while blinking back a dizzying sense of déjà vu. Her phone started ringing again; Dom calling back. She answered with a terse question. "Did you get ahold of Mom?"

"Not yet, but about the Feiney case—"

"I'm on my way to Mom's. I'll call you back once I know she's all right." She pushed the off button and disconnected the call.

At Marc's curious look, she sighed. "My brother, calling to argue. My car's in the parking garage. Level three."

"I'm in level one."

This stopped her short. "Are we going to have a pissing contest with every decision? If so, we'd better part ways now."

"No." He gave her a slow once-over. "They issued me a vehicle. On the off chance Feiney knows what you drive, maybe we should take that."

Made sense. She felt her face flush. They both knew there was a good possibility Feiney had a complete report on her. Where she lived, the names of her friends and family, what she drove. Any information was obtainable these days, even from inside prison, with the right person and an Internet connection.

"Sorry. You're right. Where's your car?"

He pointed. "It's parked at ground level in the garage, near the elevator. Let's go."

Uncomfortable and hating feeling that way, she took off at a jog. Despite his size, Marc easily kept pace with her. When they reached his car, a standard issue, navy-blue sedan that screamed law enforcement, he used the remote to unlock the doors. She slid inside and buckled up without looking at him.

The odd sense of attraction and uneasiness continued to make her feel both uncomfortable and furious. She spent a lot of time angry these days, something her therapist claimed to be working on. The way she looked at it, resentment was a hundred times better than self-pity. Anger fueled her, kept her going on days when she wondered why she bothered to get out of bed.

"Where to?" he asked.

"I'd feel better if you'd let me drive."

"I'm familiar with the area," he chided. "Give me the address and I'm sure I can find it."

Whatever. Still slightly uncomfortable, she shifted in her seat and rattled off the address.

Without another word, he pulled out and headed toward the freeway. He had the radio tuned to a local country music station. Telling herself to relax—not easy when her mother might be danger—she concentrated on watching the traffic.

Only the music filled the car as he drove. Grateful that he didn't feel the need to engage in pointless chatter, she ran through various scenarios in her head. Having a plan of action always helped, especially when one was as emotionally involved as she.

Exiting I-635, they pulled up in front of the well-kept, brick ranch house shaded by huge oaks and purple crepe myrtles. The place looked like it always did—immaculately cared for, with a perfectly manicured lawn of lush Saint Augustine grass. The windows sparkled in the sunlight. Nothing looked out of place.

She took a deep breath, clearing her mind and trying to look at her childhood home objectively. If Feiney had been here, he could have gone in through the garage or busted out a window in the back. Worse, he could have followed Lillian Cordasic in and, even now, might be inside.

The idea sent a chill through her.

"You ready?" Marc looked intent, focused.

Heart pounding, she nodded. Drawing her weapon, she exited the car and headed to the left side of the garage. He did the same, taking the right. Moving quickly and keeping a low profile, they canvassed the sides of the house. Again, they found nothing out of the ordinary. The grass had been recently mowed and the flower beds were undisturbed. A six-foot-tall cedar fence enclosed the backyard, keeping unwanted intruders out.

Marc joined her as she tried the gate. Locked.

"No way anyone got in here."

"That's a good thing," he murmured.

"Yes. She always keeps this locked." Worry coiled tight inside her chest, making breathing difficult. Again she drew upon her simmering irritation, chasing away the fear

"We need to go inside."

"Let me try calling her again." Digging her phone from her pocket, she hit redial. The call went straight to voice mail. "Her cell is still off."

"Try the house."

She did, hearing the sound of the phone ringing inside. Finally, the answering machine picked up and she disconnected the call.

"No answer. Where the hell is she?"

He gave her a long look. "Do you want to call for backup?"

"No. I don't want to get the locals all riled up unless we have to." Digging in her pocket, she produced a key. "This is to the front door. Are you ready?"

"Of course." As she met his blue eyes, a jolt went through her. Damnedest thing.

"You know, if Feiney was here, he'll have left something to let us know."

*That* was something she didn't want to see, or even think about. Again she had to tamp back the emotions. "So help me, if that bastard has touched one hair on my mother's head…" Though prayers had never helped her in the past, she found herself muttering a quick one under her breath, too low for Marc to hear.

At least he didn't give her any of the usual platitudes. If he'd told her everything was going to be all right, in that particularly low, level voice men sometimes used to talk to hysterical women, she would have had no choice but to hit him.

Unlocking the front door, she leaned in. "Mom?" No answer. But then she hadn't really been expecting one.

Once inside, she and Marc checked out every room, side by side, guns still drawn. Like partners. A weird feeling she wouldn't allow herself to dwell on. Instead, she viewed everything with an impartial eye, trying for the professional detachment she'd once been so good at invoking. Elegant furnishings, polished wood. Quiet and perfect. Everything looked normal, impossibly neat and as unlike her own chaotic apartment as it could possibly get.

Nothing. Not one single item appeared out of place.

"She's not here." Marc touched her arm and she jerked away. Purely reflex.

"Sorry." Though he'd no doubt meant to be reassuring, physical touch was the last thing she needed right now.

Except her mother's, of course. She wanted her mother. Tragically, Lea knew intimately what Feiney would do if he'd captured her. The Cowtown Killer didn't believe in quick and merciful killings. No, he liked to drag out his torture, along with cruel, humiliating sex.

Wincing, she closed her eyes, trying to will away the images, allowing the familiar—and oddly comforting— anger to fill her instead.

"Hey." Marc touched her again, this time ignoring her resistance and slinging his arm across her shoulder to pull her into his side. "Take it easy, Cordasic. She's not here and there's no sign of forced entry. None of Feiney's glaring clues. The place looks completely normal. Don't torture yourself."

She nodded. "You're right. There's no sense in imagining anything when I don't know for sure what happened."

"Exactly. Deal with what you do know for now. That's the best way you can help your mom."

Clenching her jaw, she nodded. Though she knew she should, this time she didn't pull away. He saw her as fragile, which she hated. The only time she'd ever been like that was when Feiney had kept her bound and brutalized. She'd sworn never to be anything even remotely resembling fragile ever again.

"Feiney is dangerous," she said, stating the obvious.

"I know. That's why we're going to catch him."

His choice of wording got her attention. "*We're?* I still haven't decided on this whole working together thing."

"Later." Releasing her, he crossed to the bay window and peered out. "Let's locate your mother first. Call her again."

Without comment, she hit redial. Again, the call immediately went to voice mail. "Nothing. Still no answer."

"She must have turned off her phone."

"She never does that." Meeting his gaze, she let him see the fury in her own. "I'll reiterate. If that madman took my mom, all bets are off."

One corner of his mouth lifted. "Sugar, all bets are already off."

*Sugar?* For a moment she stood frozen, staring. Then, shaking her head, she did one more hopeless check of her phone, just in case her mother had left a voice mail or something and she'd missed it. Nothing.

She went to the laundry room and opened the door to

the garage. Empty. Relief flooded her. Slowly, she turned to look at him. "Her car's gone."

"See?" Holstering his gun, he nodded. "She's out somewhere. Now all we need to do is locate her."

"Yeah. But I won't feel better until I see her for myself and make sure she's all right. She always has her cell with her and it's always on." Once again, she hit redial, listening as the call again went directly to voice mail.

"Still no answer." They both were aware that Feiney could have snatched her while she was out shopping.

"I'm sure she's fine." Expression inscrutable, he crossed to the window. "I'm thinking Feiney couldn't have resisted bragging if he actually had her. You would have heard from him by now."

Oddly enough, this reassured her. She let out a breath she hadn't even been aware of holding and nodded. To keep herself busy, she began a second search of the house, focusing on the kitchen and the master bedroom. This time, she hoped to find some clue as to where her mother had gone.

The sound of the garage door going up made her freeze. She hurried back to the living room.

"Is that her car?" Marc pointed out the bay window as a red Mini Cooper pulled into the driveway.

"Yes!" She ran to the garage, impatiently waiting for her mother to finish pulling in.

The car door opened and Lillian Cordasic climbed out, a broad smile on her face. "Lea, what are you doing here?"

"Where were you? I called your cell several times and you didn't answer."

Slowly, Lillian's smile faded. "I was working out at the gym." She frowned. Lea realized her mother wore workout clothes and had her normally well-coifed hair in a ponytail.

Lillian cocked her head. "What's going on?"

Glancing at Marc, Lea took a deep breath. "You're going to hear about this on the news anyway. I'm surprised you haven't already. Feiney's out."

"Out? What do you mean? How is that possible?"

Marc stepped forward. "He escaped Huntsville. Both the FBI and the sheriff's office are looking for him."

"And you are?"

Marc held out his hand. "Marc Kenyon, Tarrant County Sheriff's Office."

Shaking it, Lillian met his eyes. "You're the one who rescued my daughter."

"Yes."

"And you're protecting her now."

"Not protecting, Mom," Lea cut in. "We're working together to recapture Feiney."

Marc shot her a look, but didn't comment.

"Are you sure that's wise?" More than anyone, her mom realized what a toll the kidnapping and subsequent medical leave had taken on Lea. And she didn't even know the half of it.

"I have to, Mom. Let's leave it at that."

After a long pause, Lillian nodded. "We'll discuss this later."

No, they wouldn't. Lea meant to make certain of that. "I talked to Dom. He wants you to go to Vegas to visit him and Rachel."

"I won't leave you alone. Especially not now."

Knowing how much her mother detested scenes in front of strangers, Lea sighed. "Somehow I knew you'd say that."

"Mrs. Cordasic…" Marc focused his baby blues on

her mother. "We have reason to believe your life is in danger."

Coolly, Lillian looked back. "I'm more worried about my daughter. That lunatic will go after her."

"Mom." Lea put her arm around her mother's slender shoulders. "Feiney's not above using you to get to me. If I have to worry about you, I won't be nearly as effective."

"I don't care about effective. I'll go to Vegas if you'll go with me."

"I can't do that." Frustrated, Lea moved away. "You know I can't do that."

"I know nothing of the sort."

"Mom, Dominic will be calling at any moment to invite you. Please give his invitation to visit Vegas some serious thought."

"Dominic wanted to come here, too, didn't he?" Her mother was very perceptive where her children were concerned.

Frustrated, all Lea could do was nod.

"That settles it. I'm staying." Glancing at Marc, Lillian gave a determined smile. "Would you like something to drink? Coffee maybe? I baked one of my favorite cakes for the bridge game tomorrow, but I can always bake another. Would you like some?"

"We can't stay, Mom," Lea said, not giving Marc a chance to answer. She shook her head for emphasis as Lillian started toward the door. "We've got to get back to the office."

"I understand. Will you promise to come have supper within the next week? The sooner the better."

Dutifully, Lea promised. Her cell phone chirped as they headed to the car. She had a text message.

From Feiney.

# Chapter 3

Shoving the phone back in her pocket, Lea moved briskly.

Back in the car, Marc glanced at her as he turned the key.

"Well?"

"Feiney sent me a text."

"What's it say?"

She looked uncharacteristically hesitant. "Ah, jeez. I really don't want to tell you."

That made no sense. "Why not?"

She shook her head.

"Let me see it." He threaded his voice with steel. "Or tell me. What'd he have to say?"

Still she hesitated. Finally, she handed him the phone.

He powered up the display. *"Guess where I am now?"* he read aloud.

"'Visiting a special girl's grave, sweetheart. Your predecessor, the one that died when you came to take her place. And I'll stop by the other two graves, too. I'll be sure to leave them some daisies, since they were always your favorite.'"

"That SOB," Marc said, his stomach churning. "This is below the belt, even for him."

"There's nothing he won't stoop to doing. You know that."

"Reading this makes me want to hit something. Anything, as long at it breaks." His voice shook.

Lea stared at him. "You know, maybe we have more in common than I thought."

He let that statement go. For now. Clenching his fists, he glared at the traffic outside. "That sorry sack of..."

With a squeal of tires, he yanked the wheel and wedged his car in between two cars in the lane to the right. Horns honked as the other drivers tried to avoid them. Furious, he cut over to the shoulder and accelerated, stomping down the gas and sending them careening toward the Hillcrest exit.

"What the hell are you doing?"

He shot her a shuttered glance. "Heading toward the cemetery. That son of a bitch had better not defile those girls' graves. Their families have been through enough."

"You know where they're buried?"

"Of course. Three of them are in the same cemetery. I visit their graves every so often."

Because they were the ones he hadn't been able to save.

"He won't be there." Lea crossed her arms. "But his flowers will. He knows daisies make me want to puke."

"Because he brought them to you when you were his

prisoner." While she had recuperated, Marc had studied her case, haunted by the shell-shocked woman he'd carried out from hell. Feiney had held her prisoner for two weeks, leaving scars Marc could hardly bear to think about.

Because of him. If he hadn't failed her... He cut off the thought, concentrating on driving, wishing he had his own patrol car—complete with siren and lights rather than the undercover sedan.

"It takes twenty minutes to get there," she pointed out, an odd hitch in her voice. "Feiney will be long gone by then."

Suddenly, he knew why. "You don't want to see the flowers, do you?"

"No, I don't," she admitted.

Drumming his fingers on the wheel, he braked to avoid a slow truck. "You can wait in the car. I want those flowers off those graves."

"You do realize he's playing a game, don't you? He's pulling my strings like I'm his puppet." Bitterness colored her tone. "Right now, he's got the upper hand."

"Not if you refuse to play." Though he'd spoken off the top of his head, he realized he'd spoken the truth. They didn't have to let Feiney jerk them around.

"What do you mean, refuse to play? How can I do that?"

"Simple. By not doing what he wants. He wants us to go to the cemetery. You're right, we shouldn't."

"And what will that accomplish?"

"Drawing him out. If we can make him react to us rather than the other way around, we'll be in control. If we're in control, we stand a much better chance of capturing him."

Silence again while she chewed on that. "What about

the graves?" she finally said. "I tend to agree with you—I don't want that bastard's daisies anywhere near there."

"We'll call the cemetery office and get them to remove the flowers. I guarantee, if we don't react, Feiney will call us again much more quickly."

"You may have a point," she conceded. "Except for one thing. Marc, there is no *we*. You're on the team, I'm not. Anything I do, I'm doing on my own."

He decided to let that statement go. "Why won't your mother leave?"

She sighed. "My family's been in law enforcement for generations. My mom expects danger and thinks she can somehow protect her children. Both my brothers live out of town, but I'm the youngest."

Drumming her fingers on the dashboard, she grimaced. "I've got to get her out of town. I don't want to take a chance that Feiney will try to hurt her. She's my only family member here locally and she's alone. She's the only vulnerability I have."

"Why not have her taken into protective custody? She'd qualify."

She sighed. "Because she'd refuse. I know her."

"And you're positive she won't go to Vegas?"

"Yes. There's no way she'll leave unless I go with her."

"Maybe you should consider it," he suggested.

"Don't start. If you really believe I could do that, you and I can never be partners."

He gave her a long look. Finally, he nodded slowly. "I know what you mean. Sorry."

"Apology accepted." Then she actually smiled.

He took that as encouragement. "Hell, I have to admit, I'd do the same thing," he said. "You're determined to throw yourself back into the fray, whether or not you have the Bureau's blessing, aren't you?"

Though she didn't respond, the stubborn set of her chin gave her away. Despite warnings, she wanted to confront Feiney, face him down and win. Part of him had to admire that.

The other part found it sheer madness.

Yet he'd been fully aware of what she'd do when he'd decided to help her.

Traffic slowed to a crawl.

"Does that mean we'll be working together?" he asked.

She glared at him. "I guess so."

Her grudging capitulation made him laugh.

"I'm glad you think it's funny," she snapped.

He sobered instantly. "Do you know how long it's been since I laughed? Really laughed?"

"Sorry." This time, she touched him, the gesture meant to comfort. The touch made him yearn for more, a desire so strong, so foreign—so *wrong*—that he suddenly jerked away. His elbow connected painfully with the door as she looked at him with surprise.

"Don't," he said, his voice sharp. Then because he wanted to be honest, he *needed* to be honest, he softened his tone. "Sorry."

She nodded and said nothing, making him feel worse. Around her he felt like a wire stretched to the breaking point. Worse, he didn't understand why. All he wanted to do was fix a bad mistake, capture Feiney and hopefully get on with his life.

Outside, I-635 had turned into a parking lot. All four lanes of traffic had come to a complete halt.

Since they weren't going anywhere now, he wasn't in

any hurry. Instead, he studied Lea while she made a call to the cemetery, asking them to remove the flowers.

"They said they'll take care of it," she said. "I got a harried secretary. She said something about having three funerals to work on today. Until I told her I was with the FBI, she acted like getting rid of the daisies was low priority."

"As long as it gets done… But she was able to confirm that someone had visited the graves?"

"Yeah. She said the groundskeepers had been talking about it." She shuddered with revulsion. "They'd never seen so many daisies in their lives. From the sounds of things, he brought a truckload of them."

"Where's he getting the resources to do all of this? We shut down his bank accounts when he went to prison."

"He told me he had people. Most likely fans he communicated with over the Internet or something." She looked over at him. "Remember, he was an electronics wizard before he got caught. Had his own Web site and everything. Someone kept it going, even while he was incarcerated."

Marc swore. "I should have known."

She settled back in her seat, crossing her arms. "What's your plan?"

Though the abrupt change in topic took him by surprise, he didn't allow it to show on his face. "Well, I hate to put it this way, but he wants you. You want him. *I* want him."

After a moment, she snorted. "You want to use me as bait."

"Don't you?" he shot back. "It's the only plan that makes sense."

"True. But I'm surprised that you're admitting it."

"I tend to agree with you that it's a workable plan." He offered her a grim smile. "And I think you know that it'll be a hell of a lot more difficult without backup."

"So I agree that with you on my side," she said, "maybe we can do this the right way, the official way. I think you should try and get me back on the team."

"No. Too much red tape." Taking a deep breath, he switched lanes. "Plus you were in that meeting earlier. You heard Stan. There's no way in hell he'd allow that."

"Are you going to tell them what you're doing?"

"No," he confessed. "I'm doing this without official sanction. We should be clear on that."

"So you're going to remain on the official team?"

"Yes."

She shook her head. "It's a fine line you're proposing to walk here. Almost like a double agent."

"Not that extreme. I can see a way I can accomplish both, can't you? Plus, I can tell you anything they learn."

Slowly, she nodded. "You're willing to work outside the law? Despite the fact that you could lose your job?"

"Yes." He took a deep breath, wondering how much to tell her. "I'll do whatever it takes to get Feiney. I want to be the one to capture him."

Her mouth twisted. "So do I. As if that will actually make me feel better."

"You never know." How to make her understand? Dragging his hand through his hair, he considered her. Even now, especially now, he found her beautiful and infinitely desirable. He'd wanted her back before he'd blown it and, even though he knew he was the last person she'd ever want, he couldn't seem to help how he felt about her.

"If you put it on paper, in black and white, it doesn't make sense," she mused, oblivious to the turmoil inside him.

"Yes, it does. You were wrong about one thing back in the meeting. There *is* one other person who wants Feiney as badly as you do. Me. I want the bastard so bad I can taste it."

"You sound as if it was personal for you."

He shrugged. "Maybe it was." More than she knew.

Staring out at the sea of traffic, she said nothing. When she spoke again, she changed the subject. "We still need some sort of plan. We can't just sit back and let the team try to catch him while we do nothing."

"I agree. Using you as bait is the best idea we've had so far. We need to make Feiney come to us. Hell, he's already declared he plans to get you back."

"True," she agreed. "But it's a cat-and-mouse game to him. We can't make it too easy, or he'll suspect something is up. And if we make it too difficult, there's a chance he could try for my mother. Not to mention the public we have to protect."

"The FBI and the police will be all over that. I think we can leave protecting the public to them. We're only two."

"True," she concurred in a neutral voice.

"And about making it too difficult… Personally, I think Feiney would relish the challenge. We just have to come up with a foolproof plan."

Since they both knew there was no such thing, she didn't comment.

While he negotiated the traffic, finally exiting at Hillcrest, she sat silently.

"I've thought about it." Lea lifted her chin. He was beginning to recognize the gesture. "Maybe this will work. But you can't get in my way."

"Agreed."

She peered at him, still suspicious. "I swear, if you have some master plan—"

"Like what?"

"Like trying to protect me. I can take care of myself."

"No doubt. But my only plan is catching Feiney. That's all I want." But how would she react if he were to tell her he wanted to make certain the bastard never touched another woman again? Would she share the sentiment?

She studied him, letting her gaze trace over his features. "You know what? I believe you."

"You should." He didn't crack a smile, well aware of how fragile the ground was where he stood.

For the space of a heartbeat, she hesitated. As the silence stretched out, he held his breath.

"Okay, then." She held out her hand. "Partners."

Finally, he could exhale.

Keeping one hand on the wheel, he gave her fingers a quick squeeze and flashed her a small smile. "Thank you."

"Do you have anything specific in mind?" she asked.

Straight to the point. He liked that. A girl after his own heart.

"I do. Or at least I have the beginning of an idea. First, I'm moving in with you. Or you can move in with me, your choice. But I really think we should stay in the same space."

Her eyes narrowed. "Why?"

"Again, to better the trap." He took a deep breath. "I want to be on-site when Feiney comes for you."

"What's the cover story? As you said earlier, no doubt Feiney's been keeping tabs on me."

He kept his voice as matter-of-fact as hers. "Boyfriend-girlfriend."

"He'll know I haven't been with anyone since…"

He understood. "It'll be a new relationship. One that developed as a result of his escape. You were afraid, you turned to me."

"The one who rescued me." She nodded. "You know

what? It just might work. Do you think Feiney will buy it?"

"Why shouldn't he? I was first responder. I visited you in the hospital. We could have struck up a relationship, even if it was only friendship."

The fact that they hadn't had been one of his greatest regrets. He'd loved her from the moment he saw her. Though he'd never had parents or brothers or sisters, she made him want what he'd never had, a family. But she despised him. That hurt, yet he could understand. He'd hate him, too, if he were in her place. He'd completely let her down. A debt he could only try to repay.

"True. We could have become friends." She sounded surprised at the idea, as well she should. "I guess."

Not trusting himself to speak, he raised a brow.

"Don't take it personally," she clarified. Then, shaking her head, she appeared to catch herself. "Actually, the truth is, it *was* personal. Sorry."

"Because when you look at me, you think of him."

She swallowed, loudly enough for him to hear. "Yes."

"Maybe if we get him, that will change."

"Maybe." She didn't sound too sure. But then, she had no idea what he planned to do.

"Back to the plan. My place or yours?"

She gave him a tense, tight-lipped smile. "We'll stay at my place," she said. "I'm more comfortable there and it will seem more normal to Feiney."

He continued to keep his expression impassive. "Excellent idea. Especially since he probably is aware of where you live."

"No doubt." She thought for a moment. "You need to bring some stuff. If he searches the house, he won't find men's things. That could be a problem."

"We'll stop at my place so I can grab some clothes."

"And a toothbrush."

Traffic remained at a standstill. In the distance, sirens wailed.

"Must be a bad accident." He'd never been one to wait patiently and hated both traffic and crowds. Part of being one of several kids crammed into a single room at various foster homes. But sitting in the car with her, the jangling inside him had quieted. Remarkable, and something he didn't understand.

Her cell phone chirped again. Another text.

You only think I've taken what matters. But I haven't even gotten started.

"Jeez." She snapped the phone shut. "More vague threats."

A chill filled the air. Both knew exactly what Gerald Feiney was capable of.

Finally, they neared an exit.

"Where to now?" he asked.

"I think we should go back to the FBI offices."

Unsurprised, he kept his relaxed posture. "Having second thoughts?"

"About working with you? No, not really. First, I need to pick up my car. And second, you *are* on the team. You know as well as I do that they're having strategy meetings now. You'd better get back there before they start looking for you."

"They won't be. Their office is working with mine, but separately. They've simply agreed to keep me apprised of any developments."

"And you've agreed to do the same?"

"Exactly. Though, as I'm sure you know, the FBI has infinitely better resources than I do."

"That might be true, but I'm thinking you can make an educated guess as to his next move."

He gave a slow nod, knowing she wouldn't like his answer, but also aware that on some level she had to be expecting it. "He's been cooped up in prison for six months. He'll kill someone, if only to get his sense of power going again."

She drew her breath in sharply. "That's what I thought. How long until he makes a move?"

"Soon. Maybe tomorrow. Maybe even tonight. He'll grab someone as soon as possible. The media's already been alerted."

And as usual, the public would ignore the warnings.

"And my office will have people staking out the bars as well, right?" she asked.

"I'm sure they will. But he seems to have a sixth sense about spotting undercover operatives."

"Yes, he does," she agreed. "After all, he knew who I was when he grabbed me."

"They don't expect him to deviate from his prior M.O."

Her grim nod told him she agreed.

"We've got to stop him," she muttered. "The sooner the better. Before he tortures any more women."

"We can start by getting set up. Instead of going by the office first, how about we swing by my place, then yours. My gut tells me Feiney is watching us. I'd like to get a feel for things ahead of time."

"What about my car? I'll need to pick it up."

"Let's leave it there for now. We can get it later."

Her heavy sigh told him what she thought of that idea. "And that way there's less chance of me doing anything on my own, right? Let me tell you right now, I'll need my car. We might be working together, but I'm not going to be dependent on you for anything. *Capiche?*"

"Got it."

"Fine." She settled back in her seat. "Then let's go by your place and then mine. We'll pick up my car before the end of the day."

"We're nearly there." He allowed himself the smallest smile. "That's why we exited Hillcrest. I'm over by Medical City."

She nodded, seemingly unconcerned.

He lived in an apartment a few blocks from the hospital. The brick building was ordinary, so similar to others in the area that he sometimes wondered if they had all been designed by the same architect and built by the same construction company.

Lea said nothing as he parked.

"You want to come up?"

She shrugged. "Why not."

Following him to the first-floor apartment, she stood back while he unlocked his door. He held it open and stepped aside, meaning to allow her to precede him, when something caught his eye.

As she was about to go in, he used his arm to block her and push her aside.

"Hold off." Drawing his weapon, he watched while she did the same. "Someone's been inside my apartment."

"One, two..." They moved as one, as though they'd long been a team used to working together. "Police!" Marc shouted.

A thorough search of the apartment turned up no one.

"Someone has obviously trashed the place," Lea said. "Either that or you live like a complete slob."

"I don't. I swear to you, I didn't leave it like this." Dragging a hand across his jaw, he looked like he'd like to hit something.

From her expression, he could tell that she recognized his tone. Pissed and frustrated.

"Is anything missing?" They'd already completed one circuit of the property.

"No. At least not that I can tell, which means nothing major." He slammed a pillow back on the couch. "If it was Feiney, you'd think he'd have left some sort of message."

"Exactly what I was thinking. Maybe we just haven't found it yet. Let's go through each room again."

They did, but nothing obvious presented itself.

"Done," she announced, sounding as unhappy as he felt. "You know, it might not have been Feiney."

"No, but then why isn't something missing? Plasma TV, still here. Bose stereo and speakers, untouched. Even the stash of cash I keep in my sock drawer is still there."

"You keep cash in your sock drawer? And you're a cop?"

He shrugged. "I'm also human. It's my emergency money. Where do you keep yours?"

"In the bank."

"Oh." For a moment they simply stared at each other. He had the strongest urge to kiss her, which he of course resisted. No sense in ruining the fragile truce they'd built.

"I need a beer," he said, his voice as strained as if he spoke through clenched teeth. "Want one?"

He'd bet she rarely drank, well aware of how easy it

would be to fall into that route of escape. Still, this had been one hell of a day.

"Sure."

In the kitchen, he opened the refrigerator and re-coiled.

"Damn, I just found it. Feiney's message."

## Chapter 4

"What is it?" Crowding close, she steeled herself for the sight of whatever bizarre talisman Feiney might have left.

Stepping aside, Marc let her see for herself.

Inside the fridge, in a large, ziplock bag, was a woman's severed hand, rings still on two of the fingers. One ring was a large, glittery amethyst set in platinum; the other, diamonds and yellow gold. The hand was covered with blood so red it appeared fake.

Only this was real. Some poor woman had lost her hand—and no doubt her life—to Feiney mere hours after his escape from prison.

"It's horrible."

"Yeah." Marc touched her shoulder, the lightest of touches, making her want to curl into his hand and take the offered comfort. Instead, she sensibly did nothing, just continued inspecting Feiney's bizarre and bloody gift, reaching deep inside to obtain her professional detachment.

"He's already grabbed someone," she said, turning to Marc. "What have you heard? Who all knows about this?"

"No one. The team has started monitoring missing person reports. There have been no reports of white females in their mid-to-late twenties disappearing from Fort Worth."

"Yet," she said, her tone dark, "you know and I know it's just a matter of time now." She gestured at the bloody hand. "Obviously."

"But another question is why? Why here, why me? How did he even know about me and where I live?"

"And what's the significance of the hand?"

Phone already out, Marc dialed and talked quickly. Closing his cell, he grimaced. "Forensics is on its way. The guy I spoke with is going to notify Stan."

Standard procedure. But this wasn't normal Feiney behavior.

"Man, I wish I could touch that and inspect it." But she couldn't. They both knew better than to taint the evidence.

"Why?" He regarded her curiously. "What do you think you'd find?"

"This isn't normal. Why'd Feiney give this to you? What kind of message is he trying to leave? Assuming it *is* Feiney."

"Who else would it be?" Marc made an impatient gesture. "I know we can't assume anything, but I can't think of any other whack job out there who'd break into someone's apartment, steal nothing and leave something like this in the fridge."

He had a point. Still…

"Look, we both know that Feiney always takes something from his victims," she began.

"Yeah, and quite often it's a body part."

"True. But he keeps them for trophies. He doesn't give away his trophies. Nor does he warn his potential victims."

"I'm not a potential victim." Following her train of thought, Marc shifted his weight.

"No, but I am." Again she examined the grisly offering as well as she could without actually touching it. "But why the warning? And what exactly is he trying to say?"

"It's a left hand. She's wearing a wedding ring, along with another ring. I assume the rings have some significance, or he wouldn't have left them."

"I agree." She glanced up at Marc, wondering why she, who couldn't stand to be crowded by a man, any man, didn't mind so much when he encroached on her personal space. She didn't understand how this could be, but the only explanation she could come up with was because they'd decided to be working partners.

Before the incident with Feiney, she'd made one of the best partners the Bureau had to offer, excelling in undercover work. Now, on her involuntary medical leave, she wondered if she'd ever work undercover again.

"Too bad he used plastic. That dilutes a lot of the DNA evidence."

"I don't doubt that he knew that, but even if he didn't, putting the hand inside a paper bag wouldn't have the same oomph." He shot her a sideways look.

That remark nearly made her smile. She'd always had a well-developed sense of gallows humor. Nearly all frontline law-enforcement people did. It was either that, or go stark raving crazy.

Meanwhile, a forensic team was en route to gather evidence. "I'd better leave."

"No. Until Feiney is caught, I don't want to let you out of my sight."

Dumbfounded, she stared at him. "What are you talking about? That sounds like you *are* protecting me. Like I said before—I don't need a bodyguard... I need a partner."

"And that's what you've got. But be reasonable, Cordasic. Feiney's obviously been here. He wants you. If I'm not around when he makes the attempt to grab you, we'll never catch him."

She lifted her chin. "And you don't think I'm capable of defending myself?"

"On the contrary, you're more than capable. Just maybe not up against him, okay? We agreed to tell each other the truth, so I'm putting this out there right now." He released a breath. "He messed with your head—hell, he messed with mine. You need me to watch your back."

Coolly, she raised one brow. "Are you done with the psychoanalysis?"

A reluctant attempt to smile tugged up one corner of his well-shaped mouth. "Yeah. Sorry."

"Apology accepted."

"Are you always such a hard-ass?" Marc murmured.

If he only knew. "I grew up with two older brothers. I learned early on how to take care of myself."

He glanced at his watch. "Forensics should be here at any minute."

"I'll stay in the background. If they talk to me, I'll just be casually friendly. The FBI's a big office. Though I know most of them, I don't know every single body in the crime scene investigation unit."

He nodded, his expression somber. They both knew there was a strong likelihood she knew someone on this team. But if she played it right, no one would have any suspicions.

"No mention of Feiney," he said.

Relieved, she gave him a tense smile. "My thoughts exactly."

"And since this is my place, I'll have access to whatever they learn about the hand."

"You'll have to tie it to Feiney sometime, you know," she reminded him.

"I know, just not with you here."

A few minutes later, the forensic people arrived. After exchanging a quick nod with the two-man team—guys she'd worked with in the past—Lea moved to the living room. She listened as Marc explained about the break-in. With him working closely on a high-profile case, he hadn't wanted to call the local police in, so the FBI people were sent instead.

Though they nodded, the CSI guys were focused on their work. After the obligatory photographs, they cataloged and removed the evidence.

Only when they were finished did one of them—a forty-something guy with a handlebar mustache—address Lea.

"Didn't know you and Kenyon were friends?" he said, making the statement into a question.

Rather than answer, Lea settled for a noncommittal smile.

A few minutes later, the FBI men left.

"Let me pack a few things and we can be on our way," Marc said.

"Okay." Lea followed him into his bedroom. "I have to tell you, I'm a little worried about what we might find at my place after this."

He paused in the act of pulling a large duffel bag out of

his closet. "Do you think he broke into your place while we were here? Kinda risky."

"I know. And realistically, I don't think so," she said. "This message was for me. If I could only figure out what he's trying to say."

"We just need to let it stew awhile. I'm sure something will come to us."

Nodding, she watched as he methodically tossed clothing into his duffel. She perched on the edge of his bed when he went into his bathroom to collect toiletries.

A moment later, he emerged and gave her a big thumbs-up. "All done. Are you ready?"

Slowly, she got to her feet. When he'd appeared in the bathroom doorway, she'd had the strangest urge to let herself fall back onto his bed and hold out her arms to him.

As if that was going to happen. Ever.

"Let's go," she said brusquely. "Do you want to get my car first?"

"Let's pick it up later. I want to check out your place and make sure it's secure."

The drive from his apartment to hers only took a few minutes. Miraculously, the traffic flowed and a primo parking spot was open, right near her building.

Marc parked, got out and hefted his duffel bag. She stood frozen, watching him, her mouth inexplicably dry.

When he glanced at her expectantly, she was able to make herself move in the direction of the stairs. "I'm on the third floor, so it's a bit of a climb."

Once she unlocked the door and led the way in, she refused to give in to nervous chatter. Since she didn't trust herself to stop if she started talking, she kept her silence.

Having Marc inside her apartment felt odd. She'd moved here right after the Feiney incident and had never had a man over—not even her brothers. Marc was the first. His large frame filled her living room, making the space appear to shrink.

"Do you mind if I look around?" he asked.

Grateful that he wasn't picking up any of her vibes of discomfort, she shook her head no. "Knock yourself out."

"Thanks." Again with that flash of a surfer-guy smile, he moved off. He reminded her of a big, beautiful panther as he strode from room to room, inquisitive, inspecting, touching her things with his large, graceful hands.

Those hands... Unwittingly, she wondered how those hands would feel on her body. Odd for her and completely inappropriate. Still...heat suffused her. Glad he had his back to her, she chastised herself, forcing herself to move into the kitchen and let him finish his inspection.

Watching him, she reminded herself that this was business. Only business.

Yet, business or no, Marc was the first man inside her new apartment. For the first time, she acknowledged to herself what having him here would do to her. His presence made her feel naked and exposed, through no fault of her own, which made her angry. With herself. Always with herself.

Taking a deep breath, she reminded herself that she'd do anything to catch Feiney. Even this.

When he reached her bedroom, he stopped at the door. Turning, she caught a glimpse of his face, rugged features mildly curious as he stared at her bed, and suddenly her chest went tight and she couldn't breathe.

Talk about naked and exposed. Here, in her bedroom, she had really let her meager decorating skills explode. Her bed was a sensual oasis, a swirl of colors and textures in an apartment single-mindedly devoid of them. Amethyst silk next to turquoise and cream, fringed and puffed pillows, all against one wall painted black.

And then there was the bed itself. The massive sleigh bed had been made for two and belonged to another era. When she'd found it in a small furniture shop uptown, she'd been unable to resist. She loved the swirls of darker color in the carefully polished oak, the soft curve where the sleigh bed crested and the comforting softness of the big pillow-top mattress.

Marc couldn't fail to notice. The contrast between this and the rest of her impersonal apartment was dramatic. Her bed was a decadent island in a boring, monochromatic sea.

"Nice bed," he said, his tone appreciative. She heard no laughter, nothing but a sincere compliment in his deep voice.

"Thanks." Inexplicably flustered, she turned away so he wouldn't see her face. "I, uh, turned the other bedroom into a guest bedroom-slash-office. You'll be sleeping there."

When he didn't respond, she turned to look at him.

"Are you okay?" he asked, his bright blue gaze touching on her face. The heat in his eyes, whether real or imaginary, made her shiver.

*Damn.*

"You know what, maybe this is a bad idea," she said brusquely, suddenly panicking, though she managed to keep from revealing that in her voice.

"What's a bad idea?"

"You staying here and all. Maybe we should rethink this."

He pinned her with his look. "You can do this, Lea. You won't notice I'm here, and I'm betting that it won't be that long before he makes his move."

Gritting her teeth, she faced him down, telling herself

there was no way he could know that she was afraid. "I'm counting on that," she said.

"I know this guy. I've studied him exhaustively since his conviction. I suspect you know him, too, probably even better."

Dropping this bombshell casually, he didn't wait for her to react before he turned away and began to explore the rest of the apartment, disappearing into the guest bedroom.

*Damn.*

Desperate for a distraction, she turned away and dug out her cell. Time to call Dom, to find out if he'd had better luck convincing their mother to go to Vegas.

"She won't come," Dom said glumly, answering without even saying hello. "In between the time you left her house and the time I called, she'd worked herself up into a lather."

Lea groaned. "She's furious with me, isn't she?"

"I think she's more worried than mad. Lea, she's really, really afraid."

"That's why I want her to go to Vegas," she exploded.

Silence. Then Dom's quiet voice. "She's not frightened for herself, Lea. She's worried about you."

"I'm scared Feiney will try to grab her."

"Yeah. Me, too. Though on the plus side, when she hung up with me, she said she was going to the shooting range for target practice."

Their mother had inherited their father's gun collection. She now owned several rifles, a couple of shotguns and numerous pistols. And knew how to use them. She'd even been one of the first women in Texas to get certified to receive her concealed weapon permit.

"That's something, right?"

"Maybe." Conceding the point, Dom went silent again.

But not for long. "Actually, I think she's planning to try and protect you."

Lea nearly choked. "You can't be serious. She needs to stay as far away from me as possible."

Dom swore. "What are you planning to do? And don't try to pretend that you don't know what I'm talking about."

"Nothing," she said, aware it sounded weak. "Just my job."

"Do you have a good team?"

She eyed her fingernails, noting she needed to file them again. "The best."

"All right." A former FBI agent himself, her brother knew the importance of a good team. "Be careful, okay?"

"Always." Hanging up, Lea looked up to find Marc had returned. Seeing him standing in the hallway as if he belonged, all broad shoulders and lean hips, brought a pang of…something. What, she wasn't a hundred percent positive, but she was pretty sure it was desire.

She either needed to get over it or get laid, plain and simple. She figured she'd get over it.

As if he knew her inner turmoil, Marc gave her a carefully casual smile. "Do you have a spare key?"

With an equally careful nod, she went to the kitchen drawer and retrieved her extra key. Handing it to him, she ignored the jolt of connection as their fingers touched.

Stupid, stupid, stupid. Once, she'd believed in fairy tales and love stories. No longer. There was nothing left of herself to give to anyone. Especially to him. Feiney had destroyed every iota of that part of her.

"If you want your car, let's run by the office and pick it up."

Relieved to get out of the apartment, she grabbed her purse. "Let's go."

Once she'd gotten her own vehicle, she pretended to let Marc lead the way. When he turned left, she made a right. Her phone instantly rang.

"Where are you going?"

The casual question set her teeth on edge. Not his fault, she told herself. "I need to stop at the store."

She wondered if he'd catch what she didn't say—that she needed a minute or two of alone time.

He must have, because he didn't argue. "See you back at the apartment," he said and hung up.

For a moment, she could only stare at her phone. Then, exhaling, she pulled into the grocery store parking lot. Finally, the tension between her shoulders eased somewhat.

She sat in the car for a few moments, getting a good visual on her surroundings. No way Feiney was catching her unprepared this time.

Inside, she picked up the ingredients for lasagna, something she hadn't made in forever. Suddenly, for no good reason, she craved it. She also got an inexpensive bottle of red wine.

Back at the apartment, there was no sign of Marc, but she could hear the guest bathroom shower running. Unloading her groceries, she busied herself browning sausage, boiling noodles and assembling the lasagna while the oven heated.

Usually, cooking relaxed her. This time, all she could think of was Feiney and his next hapless victim. As of yet, no one had turned up missing, and the severed hand's fingerprints hadn't brought up a match.

The shower cut off. She kept herself busy, not wanting

to look up when the bathroom door opened and, still damp, Marc went to his room.

Finally, she had the dish assembled. As she put the lasagna in the oven to cook, she realized why she'd subconsciously been craving lasagna. As a child, her mother had always cooked it when her father had completed a case.

In other words, she already wished this entire case was over. Grimacing to herself, she made a bowl of salad and got some garlic bread ready to put in the oven later.

Still no sign of Marc.

She called the cemetery again, wanting to verify that the daisies had been removed. This time the person who answered had no idea what she was talking about, though she promised to look into it.

Too restless to watch TV or read, she paced. Midway through her fourth circle around the living room, she realized she didn't want Marc to come out and see her so agitated.

Instead, because she knew eventually she would have to, she dug out the boxes she'd shoved in the back of the hall closet, brought them out into the living room and, sitting on the couch, she opened them.

Western jeans and shirts, crisply pressed and neatly folded. Two pairs of cowboy boots and an elaborately styled belt with a large silver buckle, the kind won in barrel-racing competitions. A hatbox, containing a pearl-gray Stetson hat. Cowgirl getup. Her undercover clothes, the ones she'd kept wanting to throw away but now was glad she hadn't. She'd been wearing similar clothing when Feiney had grabbed her. All of Feiney's victims had been wearing cowgirl duds when they'd died.

Even looking at them creeped her out.

She couldn't shake the uneasy feeling that things were

about to go into overdrive. Not only had Feiney managed to defile the graves, but he'd broken into Marc's apartment and put a severed hand in his fridge. She'd listened to Marc and ignored Feiney's attempt to lure her to his victim's graves. She could only imagine the murderer's reaction to her lack of response.

And they still knew nothing about his victim. Who did the severed hand belong to, and what was the significance of putting this particular body part in Marc's apartment?

Next time Feiney called, she'd have to ask him.

A few minutes later, the homey smell of the lasagna cooking in the oven beginning to fill the air, Marc walked out into the living room.

He sniffed, then rolled his blue eyes. "It smells like heaven in here."

"I made lasagna." Managing an impersonal smile back, she glanced down at her boxes.

"What you got there?" Marc came around the side of the couch. He smelled wonderful—a clean, masculine scent. He'd changed into low-slung denim jeans and a soft black T-shirt and looked, well, good enough to eat.

For an instant she wondered what might have happened if she'd met him before Feiney. She'd been a different person then. More carefree, more hopeful. An eternal optimist, her family had once called her. She'd seen a silver lining in every cloud. Feiney had changed all that.

She didn't think she'd even recognize the woman she'd once been.

Pushing away the feelings such thoughts inevitably brought, she got to her feet. "Just making sure I still have enough stuff to wear in case I end up going back undercover."

"I doubt that'll be necessary," he said. "Don't forget… we're going to make Feiney come to us, not try to lure him in public. He's already let us know how badly he wants you."

"True." Grateful and inexplicably angry again, she went into the kitchen and finished setting the table. The timer went off, and she took the lasagna out of the oven and put in the garlic bread. "But I still think we should do something. Going out and trying to make contact with him is better than sitting around waiting for him to come to us. Plus, it will help us with the couple thing."

"True. Might help to make him jealous." His hand on her shoulder made her jump. "You didn't have to go to all this trouble," he said.

"I know," she snapped, then forced herself to gentle her tone. "I was craving lasagna. It's a Cordasic family thing."

At her sudden tension, he removed his hand.

Normalcy, she thought, gritting her teeth. She could do this. She had to. The most important thing right now was catching Feiney and sending him back to prison. If she had to be civil to Marc Kenyon to do it, then she'd be civil.

"Do you need any help?" he asked.

She shook her head no, feeling uncomfortable again. Her social skills really sucked these days. Damn. She shouldn't have cooked.

"This looks wonderful but, I repeat, you didn't have to do this," Marc said, echoing her thoughts. For a second this disconcerted her, then she managed a shrug.

"Yeah, well, as I said. I wanted to. Just to make sure there's no confusion, after this you'll have to fend for yourself. I usually just eat a TV dinner and a salad. Or order a pizza."

He grinned, pulling out a chair. "Then I definitely promise to enjoy every bite."

His grin sent warmth rushing at her. She stood stock-still, not entirely certain how to react. He had a way of doing that to people, she realized. Turning away, she kept herself busy dishing out the food, hoping he hadn't noticed her blush.

Once she'd placed everything on the table, including the fragrant garlic bread, she pulled out the chair opposite Marc and dropped down into it. Coworkers, she reminded herself, pushing away the unbearable coziness. Still, common courtesy necessitated her playing hostess and she dished up a huge, steaming slice of lasagna for Marc first, before serving herself.

At first she felt awkward, the forced intimacy unwelcome and uncomfortable, but Marc's easy humor eventually relaxed her. She managed to clean her plate and even joke when he went back for seconds.

Meal finished and leftovers wrapped and stowed, they wandered into the living room, each taking an opposite end of the couch to map out their plans. Turning on the television for background noise, Lea froze as the announcer for channel four news at nine came on. The lead story was the disappearance of two women from a bar in the Fort Worth Stockyards area. Not one woman, but two.

She exchanged a stunned look with Marc.

"No one called me," he said, digging in his pocket for his phone. "Why the hell didn't anyone call?"

Her gut clenched. Battling the fear, she summoned up the familiar frustration. She wanted to throw something, break something, smash the television or even Marc.

Marc cursed. "No answer." He immediately punched in another number.

"You were right," she said, jaw aching from clenching it so tightly. "He struck again and with a vengeance. Those poor women. I wonder which one is missing a hand."

"We screwed up. Not you and I, the team." Up and pacing, Marc dragged his hand through his hair.

"I—"

But Marc wasn't listening. "No way he should have taken two. He's never done that before. Not two women. And if this just happened last night, then Feiney's been busy."

While he made his call, she watched the rest of the story. The media had already made the connection between Feiney and the women, but since the bodies hadn't yet been found, they couldn't say for sure that this was the work of the infamous Cowtown Killer. As usual, that didn't stop them from speculating. The general public was warned, especially women. Lea knew from experience that few would listen.

Closing his phone, Marc returned to the sofa as the news segment ended and a commercial came on. Lea muted the sound.

"What's up?"

"Stan and his guys are astounded. They had two decoys at two different bars. But Feiney went to JR's, the same one he grabbed you from. They didn't have a decoy there."

"Even if they did, Feiney wouldn't have gone for her. He's got some agenda."

"Which involves you," Marc stated.

She didn't argue. "Okay, so the local authorities think he snatched two women. Do we know this for sure? One of them might have gone somewhere else."

"They went to the bar together and left together. They were twins. The bartender remembers them." He sighed. "I don't know how Feiney talked two of them into leaving with him, but it appears he did."

Her heart sank. Doggedly, she refused to accept his

words. "We don't have the bodies. Maybe he didn't get them. Maybe they went somewhere to sleep it off. Maybe they'll show up in the morning."

Though Marc nodded stiffly, they both knew she was wrong.

"Are they running the fingerprints on the hand for a match?"

"Yes." Marc continued to pace. He looked shell-shocked.

Lea was familiar with the helpless, impotent feeling. "We've got to do something," she said.

"I agree, but what? The police are out in droves searching for those girls. The Feds have joined in."

She lifted her chin. "We can't let Feiney kill them. Do you have any leads? What about the bartender? Did he see Feiney?"

"No." Marc grimaced. "He's good, that bastard. Damn good."

When her cell phone rang and the caller ID showed Private Caller, it was almost anticlimactic. Feiney meant to taunt her.

"It's him. Maybe he'll give us some clue where he's keeping the women." Taking a deep breath, she punched the talk button and held the phone to her ear. "Hello."

Music bombarded her first—country music, loud and twangy. Then Feiney's voice in the background, shouting the same words he'd taunted her enough with. Cutting words, meant to demean and torment.

But not at her. It was as if he'd set the phone down, so she could listen to him and his latest victim.

Did she want to hear this? Need to? Frozen, heart pounding, she shuddered but didn't relax her grip on the phone. Through sound, he'd captured her and, once again, she was there, helpless, with Feiney looming over her, taunting her, her own body tied and drugged and unable to respond.

That poor, poor girl. A single tear slipped out and ran down Lea's cheek.

"Are you there, Lea, my daisy girl?" Feiney taunted her. "It's your last rodeo, sweetheart."

Oh God.

"Lea?" Dimly, she heard Marc's voice but, trapped in her own awful reality, couldn't focus.

She saw only Feiney's awful leering grin as he repeated the words, "It's your last rodeo, sweetheart." Which meant, in Feiney's particular lingo, that someone was going to die.

"Lea," Marc called again, his voice sharp, though she heard him only dimly. She blinked, struggling to pull herself out of the trance, but then Feiney spoke once more and she shuddered, sucked right back in.

"I've got fresh flowers, darlin'. Daisies, your favorite."

Trigger words. She dimly knew this, but couldn't seem to pull herself out of the awful place he'd sent her.

A woman screamed. Again. And again. Feeling sick, Lea disconnected the call before dropping the phone.

She hunched over, cradling her midsection, as if by doing so she could stop the blows. She knew exactly what Feiney was doing to that woman. She'd been there, experienced it, up close and personal.

Marc grabbed her, yanking her up close to him, wrapping his arms around her while stroking her hair. "You're safe," he murmured, over and over. "Safe. Hear me, Lea?"

Dimly, she was able to focus enough to nod.

She felt his hand, big and strong, lifting her chin.

Somehow, she dragged her gaze to meet his, fastening onto his blue eyes like a lifeline.

Then, he covered her mouth with his and kissed her.

# Chapter 5

Lips over hers, tasting her sweetness, Marc felt the moment when Lea came back to herself. She went from ice to fire, coming fully alive in that one instant as her frozen lips parted and she kissed him back. Mindless, heedless, as though she craved humanity and warmth after talking with a monster.

The kiss lasted only a few seconds before Lea realized and gasped, pushing him away.

Hand to mouth, she glared at him, accusation burning in her stormy hazel eyes. "What the hell?" she snarled. "What do you think you're doing?"

"I didn't think, I'm sorry," he muttered, meaning it. "I got worried when you were, er…" He couldn't even find words to describe what had happened to her.

Her narrowed gaze pinned him. "You get worried, you shake someone to try to snap them out of it. You sure as hell don't kiss them."

She made it sound as if he'd rinsed her mouth out with sewage.

Her phone rang again. This time, they both ignored it.

"Look, I said I'm sorry." He spread his hands. "It won't happen again." He gave her what he hoped was an apologetic smile.

"Don't even try that easy grin on me." Fists clenched at her sides, she balanced on the balls of her feet, looking as if she'd like to take a swing at him.

A bit of an overreaction, wasn't it? Then he understood. She was taking out on him her hatred of Feiney.

He could live with that. He'd had his own bouts of rage after she'd been taken.

"Lea, I don't know what happened. When I saw you clutching the phone with a white-knuckled grip and a deer-in-the-headlights look on your face, something inside snapped. I did the first thing I could think of to bring you out of it. Please, don't take it personally."

Don't take it personally? Right. If only he could follow his own advice.

After he'd rescued her, Marc had done some research on her.

The guys she worked with at the Bureau had, pre-Feiney, referred to her behind her back as the Iron Maiden. Nerves of steel, with a ball-busting personality. A woman who took no prisoners, rebuffed any hint of romantic involvement, and despite her beauty, wanted to be thought of as one of the guys. Most of the guys had found her aloof camaraderie a challenge and had made efforts at a little workplace flirtation, only to be quickly shot down. Rejected his entire life, Marc had never even tried.

One by one, the other guys had given up and settled for being her buddies. Over the years, her quick thinking and skilled undercover work had earned her recognition and respect.

Everything had changed when she'd gone undercover on the Cowtown Killer case and been taken prisoner. For two solid weeks, every law enforcement agency in the state of Texas had worked overtime, trying to locate her. Marc had been right there with them, his dedication tempered with guilt. After all, it had been on his watch that she'd been taken.

When he'd found her, filthy and starved, in rags and chained, he'd taken one look at her and known she was going to die. He'd been equally determined not to let her. But even then, near death, she'd been a spitfire. Instead of defeat, he'd seen rage flaring in her eyes.

That's when he knew she had a chance to pull through.

And she had.

Twice in the hospital he'd gone to see her. Too ill to talk, she'd barely acknowledged his presence. Eventually, he felt awkward and stopped going.

But he'd never forgotten her. Or came close to forgiving himself.

He thought maybe now he could atone.

If she'd let him. Now he'd gone and complicated things by kissing her.

As they faced each other down, both breathing too fast, the phone still on the floor at her feet, a text message came through. At the chime, she snatched the cell up and read the words out loud. *"'Answer this time or the woman dies.'"* Two seconds later, the phone rang again. Lea answered, putting the caller on speaker.

"What?" she snarled.

Instead of Feiney's voice, they both heard the woman

scream again, louder this time, more shrill, the sound full of anguish and fear and pain.

Lea froze. "He lied," she croaked. "She's not dead." Why she was so surprised, she couldn't say. Unless…he'd killed one woman and this was the second.

Marc moved, snatching the phone from her and taking it off speaker before putting it to his ear. The screaming had stopped—only silence greeted him. He wasn't sure if that was better or worse.

"Feiney?" he rasped. "Leave Lea the hell alone."

Again, silence.

Then Feiney spoke. "You. Tell her this—it's your last rodeo, sweetheart."

In the background, the captive gave a short scream, cut off in the middle. In the ringing silence, Feiney laughed and laughed.

Hitting the disconnect button, Marc knew Feiney's victim was dead.

From the horror frozen on her face, so did Lea.

"What did he say?" she asked.

"He repeated that thing about a last rodeo."

She blanched. "Trigger words. When he brought someone new to his dungeon, he'd say that right before he killed her in front of me."

"He made you watch?"

She jerked her head in a nod.

Marc had to clench his hands at his sides to keep from touching her, knowing she wouldn't welcome that.

Her rigid posture and the fury he saw burning in her eyes told him she was teetering on the edge.

"Crap." Bowing her head, she closed her eyes, muttering something under her breath. A quick prayer, no doubt.

Watching her, Marc did the same. Only he added a prayer for Lea. If she lived through this, he hoped she'd finally find closure, a sense of peace. For both their sakes. Without examining his own reasons too closely, he wanted her to be healed, whole.

Then, as he watched, a change came over her. Wearing what he could only describe as her cop face, she raised her head and held his gaze. "Ah, Kenyon?"

He braced himself. "Yeah?"

"We gotta get that sick son of a bitch."

"I know." He almost smiled.

"Here." Tossing him the remote, Lea rubbed the back of her neck. "It's been a long day. I'm turning in. There are clean sheets on your bed and fresh towels in the spare bathroom."

With that, she turned to go.

"Good night," he told her, his voice low. At the quiet sound of Lea's door closing, he stood and stretched.

Marc turned up the sound on the TV, and the news anchor was back to talking about the case, venturing speculation about what might have happened to the two missing women. Marc didn't need to speculate—he knew. He had no doubt Feiney would arrange the body— or bodies, if he killed both girls—as he had in the past. The media would be all over it as soon as they were found. But now, he needed to call this in. The team needed to know that the search and rescue was now a locate and retrieve.

Again, a sense of his own powerlessness filled Marc, along with its companion emotion, frustration. He and Lea had that in common, at least.

No longer able to sit still, he got up and paced. Feiney had to be stopped. The sheriff's office, the Texas Rangers and the FBI were all working on that. The law-enforcement team was doing everything by the book, but he knew they'd ultimately be ineffective. Feiney was killing again, true, but his final goal was Lea. He wanted her. He'd captured her once, against all odds, and she had the dubious honor of being the only one of his victims to survive. Thus his obsession with her. It only made sense. Marc didn't understand why the Feds couldn't see it.

The quickest way to stop Feiney before he killed again would be to arrange to let him find Lea and then take him out before he disappeared with her. This time, they'd make sure and do it right.

Not like before, when a series of small errors had let Feiney knock her out and take her from the club, all without being noticed. They'd had agents staking out the inside and the front parking lot, but none in the back, where a tiny parking lot contained a huge trash Dumpster and room for only the manager and one or two employees' cars.

And Feiney's as well, apparently.

After two weeks of fruitless searching, they'd all believed Lea was dead. Only a small miracle involving a dead woman's cell phone had enabled them to locate her and get to her in time to save her.

This time he didn't want to take a chance, so Feiney would have to be brought down. If Marc got a clear shot, he sure as hell was going to take it. He told himself he'd shoot to wound, though a small, deep, dark part of him wondered if that wound might happen to be fatal.

Since the day she'd stood in court and watched Feiney sentenced to life in prison, Lea had packed up her undercover clothes and put them away. She had not set foot inside a country-and-western bar and in fact, vowed never to do so again, if she could help it.

The mere sight of a cowboy hat made her shudder, and the thought of wearing Western boots again sent her heart rate skyrocketing and made her palms sweat.

Living in Texas, this newly developed phobia could have

made her life extremely difficult, had she traveled much outside the uptown Dallas neighborhood where she lived. Luckily for her, she no longer had any reason to venture west, toward the neighboring city of Fort Worth. She hoped she never had to again, at least not for a long, long time.

Yet here she stood, wearing boots and jeans, elbow to elbow with the rowdy crowd in the White Elephant saloon. The bar was crowded and smoky, the music loud. The Fort Worth locale attracted a variety of people, most dressed in Western gear, right down to the large silver belt buckles and cowboy boots. They mingled, danced, talked, drank and laughed, but she couldn't move. Frozen, all she could see was him.

Him. Feiney, staring right at her, pure evil radiating from the black, bottomless pools of his eyes.

Too late she realized he had a knife. He raised his hand, the long blade flashing in the smoky haze. Acting on instinct, she reached for her Glock, only to find her holster missing. Belatedly realizing she was, once again, undercover, wearing jeans and boots and way too much makeup, she leaped sideways.

Not quickly enough.

The first cut tore through her arm, deep and painful, shredding skin and muscle. The second sliced through her breast. She fell to her knees, slipping in her own blood. The pain burning so sharply, so intensely, she knew he'd finally won. This time though, she wanted him to kill her. If she had to, she'd force him to slit her throat. She'd rather die than let him take her back to that room, to keep her prisoner. She bared her throat, waiting for the final slash that would take her life....

Gasping for air, Lea woke to the sound of her own scream. Shaking, covered in a damp layer of perspiration. A dream. It had only been a nightmare. Of course.

Her bedroom door opened, the flare of the hall light making her squint. She tensed as Marc stepped inside.

"Are you all right?" He sounded concerned. "I heard you scream and…"

"Bad dream," she muttered, suddenly, overwhelmingly conscious of him. Half-naked, wearing only boxer shorts, his tanned and muscular chest gleamed in the hall light. He looked sexy as hell—too damn desirable for her peace of mind.

And this—him coming to comfort her after a nightmare—felt way too clichéd, like a badly written romance novel.

"Do you need anything?" He took another step into her room, closer to the bed, closer to her.

Suddenly, she was on fire for him. Shocked, she could only shake her head no. She wanted to burrow down under the covers and analyze her sudden need, nearly as intense as the pain in her dream. This was a first—the first time she'd been tempted to use sex to chase away the nightmares.

The first time she'd even thought about sex since Feiney.

"Lea?" He moved closer. "Is there anything I can do to help?"

Her sense of irony kicked in. This was far too melodramatic. Woman has bad dream, man shows up to comfort her and they end up making mad, passionate love.

Not her, not them. She might be many things—foolish and intelligent, strong and scared, trying like hell to be normal. But the one thing she would never be was formulaic.

So, despite her completely inappropriate desire, she croaked out a quick, "No, thanks."

As if he knew his effect on her, the handsome SOB inclined his shaggy blond head. "Are you sure?"

"Sure?" At least she had her favorite ratty old T-shirt on, not some silky scrap of do-me-please material. Even as she slid down under the covers, pulling the sheet up over her throat, she lifted her chin. She might be grappling with a few issues, but she was not a coward.

"You know, I'd sort of started to wonder when you were going to get around to this," she sniped. "With your reputation and all, plus that kiss earlier."

"Get around to what? And what do you mean, my reputation?"

Though she had to struggle, she summoned a mocking smile. "You know. Bad boy of the sheriff's office. You're proving them right by coming on to me, you know." With Marc's good looks, women—from clerical to officers—threw themselves at him. And being male, Marc had taken advantage of the bounty so freely offered. He never allowed things to get too serious. Why, she had no idea. But if a girl wanted a good time, Marc was the go-to guy. Even Lea would have been tempted once.

She couldn't be certain in the shadowy light, but what looked like surprise flashed in his eyes. "Coming on to you? Give me a break. Worrying about my partner when she screams out in the middle of the night is bad?"

"You know what I mean," she accused.

Slowly, he shook his head.

She felt the sting of embarrassment, but held her ground. Maybe the attraction she felt zinging between them was just a figment of her imagination. All for the better, right?

He cleared his throat. "You don't need anything, then?"

"No." Feeling faintly guilty, she sighed, realizing that

maybe, just maybe, she'd judged wrong. "Nothing. Thanks for asking."

She thought that was a clear dismissal, but he didn't move. Instead, he stood over her, looking down at her. She felt his gaze burn as if he'd touched her. Heat again flooded her and she wanted to squirm.

"I'm fine," she repeated.

"No, you're not." The mattress dipped as he sat down on the edge of her bed. Too close for comfort. Suddenly, she couldn't stop thinking about that kiss earlier. That knock-your-socks-off, too-good-to-be-true kiss.

Another shocker—she still wanted him. Again. With twice as much intensity as before. All she had to do was reach out her hand and...

*Hell. No.*

"You'd better leave," she choked out. "Seriously."

Ignoring her, he leaned closer, sending her traitorous heart into pitter-patter double-time. Payback?

"You should go." She crossed her arms, a classic defensive posture. "So help me, I won't be responsible for my actions if you come up with some cheesy reason why we should make out."

"Make out?" He blinked, then grinned, white teeth flashing in the dim light. "Get your mind out of the gutter, Cordasic. We're partners. Partners don't do that to each other."

"Oh." She refused to feel small. "Then why are you still here?"

"I couldn't sleep and, when I heard you call out, I knew you weren't going to be sleeping again anytime soon. Unless you want to go right back to dreamland?"

He had a point. Grudgingly, she motioned him to continue.

"I've been thinking about Feiney. We need to ramp things up."

"No kidding."

"We've got to figure out a way to piss him off, to make him so angry that he makes a mistake."

Earlier discomfort forgotten, she uncrossed her arms. "Any ideas?"

"Not yet. But I think we need to rethink our original plan. Sending you back undercover won't accomplish anything."

"What?" She sat up so fast the covers fell to her waist. "Why not?"

"Too dangerous, for one thing. Wait." He held up his hand when she started to interrupt. "We've got to take precautions. I want to make sure there's zero chance of Feiney grabbing you."

"Look, Kenyon. I appreciate you trying to be noble and all. I had a bad dream, but so what? I bet lots of cops have nightmares. I know I did, even before Feiney."

"I'm not trying to be noble, for goodness' sake. Though I will say this—I saw what happened to you earlier when Feiney started messing with you. Obviously, what you went through at his hands still has you seriously messed up."

"Thanks for the psychoanalysis. But I'm okay. Really." Lifting her chin, she dared him to argue.

"There's no shame in having difficulty because of what he did to you." His deep voice softened, becoming vaguely sensual, making her shiver. "But to set yourself up for it again—that's crazy. I know you want him caught, but no one could live through that twice with their sanity intact."

Because he was right, she let that one go. Instead, she pointed out what to her seemed obvious. "If we don't get out there in the places he's haunting, how else are we going to force him to make a move?"

"I still think you should consider going to Vegas."

"And spend the rest of my life running? I'm a lot of things, but I'm no coward. Come on, do we have to endlessly rehash this?" She huffed indignantly. "It hasn't even been twenty-four hours since we agreed to be partners. So can the concern. I'm not going to Vegas. I'm staying here. Don't worry—I'm fine."

"What about the dreams?"

"None of your business," she shot back.

"Partners," he reminded her.

Damn. If he hadn't walked in on the tail end of one, she'd have been half tempted to lie and tell him the nightmares had stopped a long time ago. But then again, she knew she couldn't. Partners told each other the truth, always and without exception. If you couldn't trust your partner, you could end up dead.

Or worse… She suppressed a shudder.

"Low blow," she said, then immediately regretted it. "I'm sorry. Yeah, I still have nightmares." She managed a casual shrug. "You never know. Maybe facing Feiney again will help me deal with them."

"Or make them worse."

Annoyance radiated through her. "Don't do that to me," she retorted. "I need a glass-half-full kind of partner, always looking on the bright side of things. The way you are with everyone else."

Again the wry smile, a flash of white teeth in the dim light. "Been watching me?"

She groaned out loud and lobbed her pillow at him. "I dug out my old undercover Western outfits earlier today. Tomorrow I'll start haunting bars over in the Stockyards and Sundance Square. Sooner or later, Feiney will show up again and we'll get him."

Marc rolled his eyes. "That's exactly what the team is doing. I don't think he's going to go for it. Not this time. He's too shrewd." He muttered under his breath. "He'll be onto them like fleas on a dog. It's not gonna be that easy. Feiney will need more of a challenge."

"You never know," she began, then stopped because he was right. It wouldn't be easy. Catching the bad guys never was. And when you had a serial killer of this magnitude with nothing to lose… 'Nuff said.

"Then toss out some alternative suggestions," she insisted. "I'm open to discussion. Since you don't think it's a good idea for me to start hanging out in the country-and-western bars, what do you propose to do?" She sighed impatiently. "He's not going to break in here and try to grab me. That's not his style."

"I think he'll abandon his style if we make him angry enough."

"How do you propose we do that?" She moved restlessly under the covers, shocked by how badly she wanted to touch him still, even if only to shove him antagonistically. According to her shrink, getting physical with anyone in any way at all would be a breakthrough. From frozen to this. She wasn't sure which was worse.

"We need to learn more about him," Marc said, "find out what makes him tick. The next time he calls, talk to him like he's your friend. Find out what's driving him."

She couldn't suppress a shudder of revulsion. "I can tell you what's driving him. He becomes aroused by blood and death. The power of killing a woman while raping her is his biggest turn-on."

"Then we need to offer him the ultimate turn-on. Come up with something, some scenario that he can't resist."

It was mind-boggling that they were having this discussion in her bedroom in the middle of the night and it didn't appear to bother him.

"How would we know what that is?" Lea asked.

"That's what we have to find out. For whatever reason, he wants you back. What we don't know is why."

"Probably because I'm the only one that got away."

"That may be true, but I think there's more to it than just that. He has feelings for you, Lea. We need to tap into those emotions and use them to draw him to us." He dragged his hand through his already unruly hair. "We need to let Feiney himself tell us what he wants."

"And then?"

"Then we give it to him."

# Chapter 6

Instinctively, Lea supposed she knew what Feiney wanted from her, but her mind shied away from the idea. "He's given me enough hints," she said, silently cursing her hesitation. "I think he wants some sort of...relationship."

The word, once said, made her want to gag.

Marc said nothing, just continued to watch her.

"He's made several comments along those lines. He's been watching me... I belong to him—stuff like that."

"How do you feel about that?" he asked, his voice gentle.

She laughed, a bitter hollow sound that was its own answer. "Look, Kenyon. I'd really like for you to quit asking me how I feel about things and help me concentrate on getting the job done." Her voice turned to steel. "I'm done hanging back. He's already killed three girls, and now maybe two more. That's got to stop. Since he wants me, I need to make myself available."

"Go on," he said slowly.

She took a deep breath. "Next time he calls, I'm going to be the one doing the taunting. Maybe you're right. We've got to figure out what will set him off. If he wants me, he's going to have to come and get me."

"Lea." Crossing the room, he sat down beside her again. His hand on her shoulder startled her, the heat of his touch burning her skin through the lightweight fabric of her T-shirt. To her surprise and consternation, again she had the oddest urge to curl into that touch. She bit her lip to keep from groaning.

"What?" she managed.

"You need to understand…the reason I ask you how you feel about things is because I need to make sure I can count on you. If you freeze up, you could endanger both of us." He leveled his blue gaze on her. "Despite his recent killing spree, Feiney's main focus is drawing you to him so he can finish what he started. This isn't going to be pretty."

This time, she couldn't suppress a shudder. "I know." Her voice sounded flat and emotionless. Not at all as if her entire being wasn't silently quaking at the thought of encountering the evil cloaked in human skin that was Feiney. What he'd done to her… What he'd done to his latest victims…

She pushed the thought away.

"I need to be sure you can handle this," Marc continued. "Tell me. Can you?"

Staring at him, she realized she wanted to put her fist through a wall. Yet his question had validity. He was certainly within his rights to ask if she could handle a confrontation with Feiney.

Worse, she definitely owed him the stark truth, no matter how much she might not like facing it.

Instead of automatically answering with vague reassurances, she thought long and hard. Everything inside her screamed a warning to run as fast and as far away as she could. As a woman, she never wanted to see Feiney's deceptively pleasant face again.

Except for one part of her. Her career had once defined her, meant everything. The woman with a proud family history of law enforcement, the crack shot, martial arts black belt, special agent part of her demanded she finish what she'd begun. A large amount of professional pride was at stake. She couldn't allow one bad guy, even if he was the mother of all bad guys, to send her running for the hills, whipped and beaten. She'd have to draw on her insatiable anger—the very thing she'd been told she must shed—to carry her through.

If she couldn't do this, she didn't see how she could ever look at herself in the mirror again.

"Though the Bureau might be right saying that I need time to heal, I also recognize one other, very important truth."

Lifting her chin, she met Marc's gaze and held it. "If I don't do this, if I don't come back into my own now, I never will. My career will be over." She swallowed hard. "Hell, my life would be over, at least as far as I'm concerned. I'd never regain the self-respect I lost at that madman's hands."

Seeing Marc watching her, a gleam of appreciation in his eyes, she debated how much more to say, how much to leave out. One thing she could never do was admit her fear. If she did, she was certain it would consume her.

"That's why it's so important that I be the one to bring that bastard in," she said quietly. "Not you, not the Bureau's team, but me. If nothing else, I'm hoping that doing so will help me regain the self-confidence that unraveled into shreds when Feiney tortured me."

With this admission, she supposed she ought to have felt ashamed. Instead, she felt like a huge weight had been lifted from her shoulders. "I can do it, Kenyon. I promise you, I won't let you down."

His smile came slowly, but when it did, she felt validated.

"You know what? I believe you. Now we need to come up with a plan, figure out a way to draw Feiney out."

"I don't think we need to do even that much. To me, the solution is simple. We need to cut a deal with Feiney. Set up a meeting place, offer me up like a sacrifice. Trade me for the other girl."

"No." Immediately, he shook his head. "Too obvious. He'd see it coming and would do something to that girl just to spite us."

"Maybe he would." She regarded him curiously. "You sound like you think you understand him pretty well."

"Yeah." He looked away, appearing embarrassed. "What I don't often tell people is that I worked for the FBI for a while. I studied to become a profiler."

That she hadn't known. "Really? What happened?"

She could tell he didn't want to say. But she'd just spilled her guts to him and turnabout was fair play.

"I couldn't do it. I saw what it did to the other guys, the profilers. The legendary burnouts, the suicides. Constantly seeing the dark side and feeling the lack of light, of hope, wore me down. So I quit. Left Quantico, stayed in Dallas and went to work for the Sheriff's office. The pay's not as good, but the job is much better."

By better, he meant easier. She'd heard about the profilers. Every agent who worked for the Bureau knew the stories. Not liking the surge of sympathy she felt hearing his confession, she blinked.

"What about your family? How'd they feel about this change of careers."

He squinted at her. "Prying?"

"Maybe I am," she allowed. "I started thinking. You know everything about me, while I know next to nothing about you."

"Then by all means, I'll tell you. Let me give you the short version. I have no family."

Now he'd startled her. "What?"

"Yeah. I'm an orphan. I don't even know who my parents were. Until I went into the military, I never had a home, unless you count the orphanage—which I don't."

Fascinated, she leaned forward. "What branch?"

"Air Force. At eighteen years old, they finally gave me what I craved—a sense of belonging. I stayed twelve years, until I got injured by a roadside bomb in Iraq." He swallowed hard, then continued.

"I survived, my team didn't. And in case you wonder how I dealt with that, let me tell you. Not well."

"So you quit the military?"

"Yes. That incident brought the realization that it was time for me to do something else with my life. Six months later, after I got out of the hospital, I found myself back in the States, looking for another career."

"And you became a cop," she guessed.

"Exactly. I took the first position I could find, working for the Washington, D.C., police force. During my time there, I made friends with a guy who worked at Quantico, and at his urging, I submitted an application to the FBI."

"There usually is a long wait period."

"Not for a guy like me. I had special skills in the military and they couldn't wait to sign me up. I tested out as somebody who'd do well in profiling." He shrugged. "It sounded interesting, so I accepted. When I completed my training, I passed everything with flying colors and, like all the other applicants in my class, awaited my final assignment with bated breath."

She remembered those days for her class well. Everyone hoped they didn't get stuck in some awful place.

At her nod, Marc continued. "The irony of being assigned to Dallas, Texas, didn't escape me. After all, I'd grown up at the Children's Home in Mesquite, a suburb of Dallas. There, and various foster homes around Dallas, Fort Worth. The fact that I had no family or friends here made it, as least as far as the Bureau was concerned, as if I'd never lived here at all."

"Wow." That was all she could say.

"Yeah, but they were right. Though I'm not the type to become maudlin, sometimes I feel—er, felt that way, too."

Almost against her will, Lea found herself really liking him. To her, that was infinitely more dangerous than mere lust.

"Okay, confession time over." Suddenly exhausted, she pointed toward the door. "We'll talk more tomorrow. Right now, you'd better leave. I need to get back to sleep."

He stood. "All right. In the morning, let's get to work on a better plan, and some sort of timetable."

"I still think we should make the offer, just to throw him off base."

"I don't. But, like you said, we'll talk about this more in the morning."

"Good night." She sighed, then stifled a yawn. "I need my beauty sleep."

Though they both knew this was a lie—that she probably wouldn't sleep another wink that night—he went.

Surprisingly, after he left she fell into a deep, dark, dreamless sleep.

At 5:00 a.m., she came awake to the sound of Marc's cell phone ringing in the guest bedroom. It gave off a loud, futuristic shrill, worse than any alarm clock, making her wonder when he'd changed the ring tone…and why.

She heard him answer, his deep voice hoarse and froggy, though she couldn't make out what he said. Pushing herself out of bed, she stepped into denim shorts and pulled on a bra under her T-shirt.

In the bathroom, she washed her face and brushed her teeth before deeming herself ready to face the day—and him. Stomach in knots, she tried to settle her nerves, but she feared she already knew the reason for the early call.

The body of Feiney's latest victim had been found.

As she left her bedroom, she nearly collided with Marc, also headed toward the kitchen, still talking on his phone. Brushing past him, she went for the TV first, figuring the Cowtown Killer would once again be all over the news. Exactly where he wanted to be.

A commercial for a fast-food chain was on instead. A cheerful clown dressed up in a king suit, singing about a huge breakfast sandwich.

Concluding his phone call, Marc came to stand beside her, his expression bleak. "They found a body," he said, confirming her guess. "Only one, so far. They're not sure what happened to the other girl, or even if he has her."

"I knew it." She grimaced. "Though I haven't heard it on the news yet, I'll bet he's set the body up the same way he did last time. Straw cowboy hat over her face. Daisies strewn all over the body."

Marc's grim expression told Lea she was correct.

"So he's not innovating." He dragged his hand through his hair, drawing her gaze. "It's so freakin' early. You got any coffee?"

She nodded, struck again by the same uneasy sense

of intimacy she'd felt last night. "The coffeepot is on an automatic timer. It should be done anytime now."

"Good." He gave her a weary smile and returned his attention to the television. "I don't know if they've made a statement yet, but the media monitors the police scanners, so they were all over the scene. The Fort Worth P.D. was keeping them back while the investigators got their pictures and bagged the evidence. I'm gonna need to go down there."

She'd thought as much. She'd give anything to be allowed to accompany him. After the news story came on, she'd mention it and see how he reacted.

Heading toward the kitchen, she got out two mugs and poured coffee. "Cream or sugar?"

"Black."

The same way she drank hers. Carrying them into the living room, she handed one to Marc. "Here you go." When they both had steaming cups of coffee, they focused again on the TV.

"Did you ask about the hand?"

He gave her a blank look. "What?"

"The victim. Did you ask if she was missing a hand?"

"No." He cursed. "The call woke me out of a dead sleep. I didn't even think of it. I'll call him back."

Punching numbers into his phone, he waited a moment then left a message. "No answer. I'm sure he'll phone me when he gets a minute."

Yet another commercial came on, something about cavemen and bowling. Finally, the station logo and the music that announced the early morning news.

They led off with a murdered woman's body found by a Dumpster in back of JR's, a bar in the Stockyards.

The report was a sanitized version of what had happened, delivered by a perfectly coiffed woman in a purple silk suit. The police weren't releasing details, the anchorwoman said, but it was widely believed this was the work of Gerald Feiney, aka the Cowtown Killer. They'd update this supposition once they had confirmation from official sources.

The report concluded with a warning for young women to be careful when going out to bars.

Predictable stuff. Less than what she'd expected, since no mention was made of the body's disposition, which would provide a definite tie-in to the Cowtown Killer.

She glanced at Marc. "The team put a lid on it, didn't they?"

"I'm assuming they did. I didn't ask."

"I think that's a mistake. People need to know the truth."

"They warned the women to be careful." His dry tone told her he knew, as she did, how much attention the public would pay to this warning.

"But they need to be told what to watch out for," she insisted. "That way, they'll take the warning seriously."

"Maybe Stan— or the Fort Worth police chief—is afraid to cause panic. You know how that kind of thing goes."

"Yeah, I do. Unfortunately." She took a deep drink of her coffee. "They need to cause a panic. Feiney killed a lot of people. Women especially should be afraid. That way they'll be more careful."

Even though they both knew human nature. The most dire of warnings would be heeded by few, no matter the cost. It was a sad fact that citizens frequently ignored warnings and pretty much did whatever they wanted, then cried foul when something awful happened.

Which it would—she had no doubt about that. Clicking the TV off, she looked at him

Refilling his cup, he gestured at the table. "Let's talk.

You said something yesterday about coming up with a plan."

Frustrated, she jerked her head in a nod. "Yeah. You got a better one than offering to trade me for the girl?"

"No. But that's definitely out of the question. I was hoping you'd agree once you slept on it." His slow smile was like the morning sun blazing over the horizon.

Stunned, she could only stare. This was getting more and more ridiculous. Collecting herself, she yanked out a chair and dropped into it, indicating the one across from her. "Sit. Let's figure out something."

Taking a long draw from his mug, he straddled the chair across from her. "Shoot. I'm all ears."

"Like I said, we're going on the offensive," she said, and waited for him to protest. When he only leaned forward, continuing to sip his coffee, watching her over the rim of the mug, she continued. "Starting tonight."

"Define *offensive*."

"I thought we could at least scope out the bars. You know he won't hit JR's, since he dumped the body there." Feiney had been fastidious about killing at a different bar every time.

"Scoping out the bars isn't a bad idea. It's not all that good either, but until Feiney contacts us again, we can give it a shot."

"You agree?" Surprised, Lea eyed him, waiting for the other shoe to drop. "That's an abrupt about-face from yesterday."

"Yeah." He drummed his fingers on the table. "The team is staking out the bar where the two girls were nabbed. But you and I know he won't go back there. And it's most likely he won't grab another one just yet. He hasn't escalated that much."

"True." Though she knew he would, the thought of what would happen once Feiney escalated made her shudder.

"Plus we don't have a second body," he mused. "If he hasn't already killed her, he'll play with her for a while."

She closed her eyes and swallowed hard. When she opened them again, she met his gaze. "Then what's the point? If Feiney doesn't even notice we're out there, why do it at all?"

"Oh, he'll notice. Believe me. I'm sure he's keeping tabs on you."

She barely suppressed a second shudder. "I don't want to think about how. But you should know that just because he might have a captive, there's no reason to think he won't go after someone else. He kept on killing when he was holding me captive. He wanted me to help him."

Regarding her thoughtfully, he drummed his fingers on the table. "Are you thinking he might be letting this latest captive replace you?"

"I don't know." She hoped not.

"More coffee?"

She shook her head. "I haven't even finished my first cup. You go ahead."

"I drink a whole pot most mornings." His sheepish smile was just as mesmerizing as the others. She stared, bemused.

"So we agree? Tonight we're going honky-tonking?"

Peering at her over the rim of his cup, he finally gave her a slow nod. "Why not? But how do we choose the right bar? He'll be setting us up."

"It won't matter where we go, as long as we let him know we're going to be there."

"There's the rub. How do you propose we do that?"

"Oh, he'll call again." She glanced at her watch. "If only to gloat about his recent kill."

As if on cue, her cell phone rang. Shooting Marc a look that said, "I told you so," she flipped it open. Only instead of Feiney, it was Stan, ostensibly checking on her.

"Just checking to make sure you're okay. Any problems?"

This in itself was so unusual she became alert.

Marc had leaned forward, obviously hoping it was Feiney. After shaking her head to indicate no, she addressed the caller. "I'm fine, Stan. Though I saw on the morning news that ya'll just found Feiney's next victim."

"We don't know that for sure," Stan bristled.

"Come on. This is me. We both know who killed that girl."

Silence, then finally Stan cleared his throat. "Yeah. Same M.O. as last time. It's definitely Feiney."

"Let me ask you this. Was she missing a hand?"

"No. We still don't know where that hand in Kenyon's fridge came from. How'd you know about that?"

"Marc told me. Marc and I are…" She deliberately paused before continuing, knowing what inference he'd draw. "Friends."

"Friends?" he repeated blankly, as though he didn't understand the word. "Since when?"

"We've been together awhile now." Deliberately keeping things vague, she steered the conversation back to the case. "About the girl. Any leads?"

"None." He sounded glum. "What about you?"

Naturally, she pretended surprise. "What about me? I'm on medical leave."

"Right. I expect you to remember that. There's no need for you to go see the victim."

"I wouldn't do that." In fact, the thought hadn't even occurred to her. She already knew what Feiney was capable of doing. She didn't need to see it firsthand.

"Good. And I'll ask again… Do you have any information you want to share with us?"

"If I did, I'd tell Marc. He's on the team. I guess you could say he's your pipeline to anything I learn, all right?"

Another silence. She guessed he wasn't too happy, and the rancor in his voice when he spoke again confirmed this.

"All right. Take care now." Stan concluded the call.

"Wow. That was weird," she told Marc, closing her phone. "Stan was so obvious he could have shouted from the rooftop. He wanted to find out if I've learned anything he didn't know."

"Because he knows you have an in with Feiney. What about the hand?"

"It wasn't hers," she replied solemnly. "So we still don't know who it belongs to. But I'm still wondering why Stan really called."

"Making sure you stay out of trouble?"

"Maybe, though I doubt it. I'm guessing he was worried I'd show up at the morgue wanting to see the victim or something."

He looked at her curiously. "Would you?"

"No. I already know what he did to her. And there's no need, since I'm already positive it's him."

Going for a refill of coffee, Marc stopped when his phone rang. "Busy morning," he remarked, then answered.

Listening, he muttered something too low for her to hear, then concluded the call.

"More news about the vic?"

"Nope. This was even better. Come on." Setting down his coffee mug, he waved her toward the door. "We've got to go. They've spotted him."

"Feiney?" Already on her feet, she stopped long enough

to step into a pair of flip-flops, then followed Marc. "Where?"

He took the stairs down, two at a time. "A neighborhood over by Twenty-eighth Street, in Northside."

Keeping pace easily, she whistled. "Dangerous place for a middle-aged white man. Especially at this hour in the morning."

"Yeah, but he's crazy. Maybe they look in his eyes and see that and leave him alone."

"Or maybe he's staying with someone he met while in the joint. Or a girlfriend. One of those foolish lonely women who write love letters to prisoners."

"I'll run a check on that immediately." Opening his cell, he punched a number, then barked the order into the phone, never breaking stride. "If we hurry, we can beat the uniforms."

They weren't so lucky. As they exited on Twenty-eighth street, a patrol car sped past them, lights flashing. They'd barely gone three blocks when they spotted two more, both with lights but no sirens.

"Talk about announcing to Feiney that he's been seen," Marc groused, slowing down and beginning to look for a place to turn around.

Lea was having none of it. "What are you doing?"

He shot her a look of disbelief. "We can't go there now. The place is crawling with law enforcement."

"So? They don't know me from Adam."

"I'm willing to bet there'll be some Feds there, too."

She said nothing, letting him tell from the set of her jaw that she didn't like hearing this. Nevertheless, it was the truth. Neither of them could alter that.

Still, she wasn't one to give up so easily. "I'd like to at least drive by. No one will pay any attention to a car."

"Unless they've set up a roadblock. No one in or out of the area without showing ID."

Her shoulders slumped. "That sucks for us, but you're probably right. I didn't even think. Let's go home."

The second the words left her mouth, she wished she could call them back. *Home.* She tried to ignore the connotations of the word. For her, home was really her mother's house, the place she'd been raised. But Marc had no home, except for the apartment that seemed as impersonal as hers.

"Sorry," she muttered, feeling like a complete and total clod.

Big hand under her chin, he gently lifted her face toward his. "It's all right. Don't sweat the small stuff."

Looking deep within his impossibly blue eyes, in that instant she realized she had more to worry about than just Feiney. In his own way, Marc Kenyon was dangerous, too.

# Chapter 7

Until he'd met Lea Cordasic, Marc could honestly say he'd never thought about even the remote possibility of making his own home, of having a family. His career had always been more than enough. But something about Lea…

He'd never forget the first time he saw her. Contrary to what she believed, the assignment to work with her on Feiney hadn't been the first time they'd met. A frequent visitor to the FBI offices in Dallas, he'd been strolling down cubicle alley one morning and turned a corner without looking. He and Lea had collided, hard. She'd stumbled so badly that she'd nearly fallen. Acting purely on instinct, he'd caught her, hauling her up against him to prevent her impact with the floor.

Gazing down at her in the split second before setting her back on her feet, with her long-lashed, hazel eyes sparkling up at him, filled with laughter, he'd instantly realized that he understood every love song ever written. If love at first sight had seemed like a myth, an uncertain, unlikely possibility, he knew it to be an absolute truth now. And the more he'd gotten to know her, with her dryly mischievous sense of humor and her talent for finding the absurd in the daily grind, his conviction that she was The One had strengthened.

He wanted Lea Cordasic like he'd never wanted another woman. He'd fallen for her, hard. Unfortunately, in a kind of ironic karmic payback, in what he'd been told was her standard operational procedure, she regarded him merely as one of the guys. No matter what he did, he hadn't been able to generate any interest other than professional.

So he'd backed off, taking time to devise a better strategy and hoping absence would make the heart grow fonder.

Then he'd been asked to provide backup to an undercover operation and learned she was acting as bait for a notorious serial killer. He'd done his part, acting under his own agency, the sheriff's office, but in an unforeseen chain of coincidences, Lea Cordasic had been captured.

While the various agencies stood still in shock, busy slinging blame, he'd volunteered to lead the team to bring her back. Since the Sheriff's office was technically in charge of the investigation, permission had been readily given.

Two weeks, one day and seven hours after being captured, Lea had located an old cell phone that one of Feiney's prior captives had dropped under the bed. She'd made the call, leaving the line open and Marc's team had been the ones who'd surrounded the house, an ordinary brick ranch in suburban Fort Worth.

Never before or since had he felt so much like he was back in Iraq, though with one key difference. He was in love with the target, and her take-no-prisoners personality put her at greater risk.

Naturally, Feiney wouldn't give up easily. When the firestorm of bullets had started, Marc had been the first in, Kevlar vest in place, under continuous fire. He led the team inside, where two of his men had rushed Feiney, taking him down. One had suffered a gunshot wound to the leg.

Heart pounding, Marc had charged down the wooden steps and broken through to the tiny basement room where she'd been held prisoner. Blocking the others' view in order to shield her, he'd found Lea, still alive, bruised and beaten and covered in filth.

He'd been the first one to see the rusty chains around her slender wrists and ankles. She'd had huge dark circles under her eyes, a snarled and matted nest of lank hair, and when she met his gaze, the look in her eyes was haunted, tormented, similar to that of a prisoner of war.

Feiney had broken something inside her. To this day, Marc wondered if she'd ever heal. Certainly she'd never regain her lost innocence.

Now that Feiney had escaped, she'd been transported back to that terrible time. Seeing her like this ripped a huge gash in his heart. Watching Lea try to be tough killed him. Each and every time that psycho contacted her, she flinched. He wasn't even sure she knew she did. And though by some miracle she managed to always sound strong and unbothered, the haunted shadows in her eyes, reminiscent of the way she'd looked when he'd first found her, lingered.

Though she kept her shoulders back and her chin up, she had to be suffering inside. Only her fury propelled her forward, only the fire of her red-hot rage appeared to motivate her.

This he could understand. He swore to catch Feiney before he did any more damage. To Lea or to any other poor, unsuspecting girl. If he had to kill the bastard, so be it. He only hoped that when it was all over, Lea Cordasic didn't hate him. Or worse, herself.

Something was off. Lea didn't know what, exactly, but Marc Kenyon had a secret he was keeping from her. Part of her wondered why she cared. The other part recognized another wounded soul hiding underneath a veneer of toughness. Sappy, she thought to herself, but true nonetheless.

A day spent without hearing from Feiney had her on edge. "Let's go out tonight," she said. "Like we originally planned."

Marc's blue gaze pinned hers. "You mean the Stockyards? I thought we agreed that would be pointless?"

"No, you agreed. Besides, I hate doing nothing. We're dead in the water here until Feiney decides to contact us. If Feiney decides to contact us."

"He will."

"I wish I could be that certain." She sighed. "I'd feel a little more proactive if we got out. Even if Feiney doesn't see us, I'll still feel like we're doing something."

"You know it could be dangerous."

She snorted. "Yeah, maybe if we were doing a full-blown undercover operation. But with you stuck to my side like glue, how can Feiney make a move?"

His slow smile warmed her. "You're right. You sold me. We'll do it."

That night, around nine, she went into her bedroom and put on the hated Western garb, applied makeup with a heavy hand and teased her hair. When she'd finished, she looked at herself in the mirror and grimaced. Except for the haunted eyes, she looked just like any other cowgirl-wannabe, out for a good time at the Stockyards. She only wished the outfit didn't make her skin crawl.

She wondered how Marc would look. She'd just bet he made a fine-looking cowboy.

When she saw him, she realized she'd completely underestimated him. "Wow," she drawled. "Who would have thought a guy like you could cowboy up so well."

He chuckled. "Keep eating me up with those eyes, sugar, and I'll show you a cowboy."

Heat flooded her, even as she told herself it was harmless flirting, nothing more. Still, as she studied him, she knew she'd never realized a man dressed up as a cowboy could look so…hot.

Low-slung jeans, a long-sleeved button-down shirt and the requisite boots, combined with his unruly blond hair, and he looked like Keith Urban. Only better.

Her mouth went dry just looking at him. Damn. She had to cough to clear her throat so she could speak normally. "Ready?"

"Sure." The way he looked her up and down made her stomach tighten. "Wow." He let out a low whistle. "I can see you're going to have a difficult time keeping the cowboys at bay."

"Thanks." As compliments went, that was perfect. Not too personal, just one colleague complimenting another on the undercover skills. That she could deal with. She found herself actually smiling at him as they headed to his car.

The drive to Fort Worth took forty-five minutes. To get in the mood, he switched the radio to a country music station, singing along in an off-key voice.

"You might look like Keith Urban," she said, punching him lightly in the arm, "but you sure don't sing like him."

He shrugged and continued mangling the latest Toby Keith song.

Reaching Cowtown, they paid to park in a lot and walked across the street to begin their night. Though they hit three of the most popular bars, including the one where Feiney had grabbed Lea the last time, she saw no sign of her nemesis. To her surprise, once she entered her undercover mode, the fear and uneasiness disappeared, almost as if she was able to dissociate from herself. She became simply an undercover agent doing a job. Trying to catch a monster.

But the night was a complete bust. Marc in tow, Lea frequented every country-and-western bar in the Stockyards area and several near Sundance Square. Not once did she catch sight of the Cowtown Killer.

"I've had enough." She linked her arm with Marc's, taking care to smile up at him in case anyone might be watching. "I keep hoping I'll look into the crowd and see him."

"He might be staying home right now," Marc pointed out. "Until the second girl's body is found, there's a distinct possibility Feiney's home torturing her."

Swallowing, Lea closed her eyes. When she opened them again, Marc was watching her. "Like me," she said, letting her raw emotion color her voice. "Just to prove it could be done again, whenever and wherever he wants."

"Maybe," Marc allowed. They'd snagged seats at the crowded bar area in Electric Cowboy and both sipped ginger ale on ice, masquerading as something more potent. "But I actually think he enjoys the torture almost as much as the killing itself. It's a power trip for him. He got a taste for this sort of thing with you, and it feeds upon his overinflated sense of control."

"No other woman should have to go through what I did."

"I agree with you. But there's more." His troubled expression warned her she wouldn't like it.

"What?"

"His time in prison, though only six months, probably exacerbated his feelings of inferiority. His need for power now is most likely far greater than it was then."

Horrified, Lea stared at him. "You're saying you think that her torture is worse?"

"I don't know." Gaze dark, Marc stared out at the packed dance floor. "But my instincts tell me yes."

She cursed. "Then we've got to find him soon."

"We need to stay a little longer."

"And if we don't see him, we'll move on to another bar." Gone was all thought of going home.

"Hey, pretty lady." A tall cowboy leaned in, his alcohol-laden breath making her gag. "Will you do me the honor of dancing with me?"

She forced herself to smile as she held out her arms. "Of course."

The second they stepped onto the dance floor, she realized her dance partner had a severe case of wandering hands.

"Excuse me." Eyes dark with possessiveness, Marc cut in, shoving the other guy away with enough force to send him stumbling. Drunk and humiliated, the cowboy yelled obscenities, clearly wanting to start a bar brawl. Luckily, his friends led him away instead of joining him in a fight, and a crisis was averted.

Lea was both furious and oddly pleased.

"Marc," she hissed, toning down her frustration as the DJ put on a slow, romantic ballad. "What the hell was that?"

One corner of his mouth kicked up in a half smile. "Shhh. Dance with me."

"But…"

He gathered her into his arms, continuing to smile that slow, lazy smile of his. "If you want to look like a woman on the prowl for a good time, dance with me."

Unable to argue with his logic, she moved into his arms.

Big mistake. Instantly, she became aware of several things. Though at five-eight, she considered herself tall, while in Marc's arms she felt positively tiny. If she allowed herself to rest her cheek against his chest and close her eyes, she could not only smell the scent of soap and male skin, but feel the strong, steady beat of his heart.

As he swung her around, his arms tightened, keeping her close. Panic flooded her, an instant of raw fear which she quickly tamped down. He was solid and muscular, unmistakably male. And she realized how badly she really wanted him.

Finally—too soon, too late—the song came to an end. Reluctantly, or so it seemed to her, he moved away, taking her arm to lead her back to their seats at the bar.

Once there, he vanished, taking care to appear only as part of the crowd, leaving her to sit alone. Though they'd done this exact scenario at several bars, as of yet nothing worthwhile had come of it.

A gum-chewing waitress arrived with a tray and a drink. "For you, hon. From the guy in the bright blue shirt, there at the bar."

Instantly on alert, Lea swung around, struggling to seem only casually interested.

"Which guy?" she asked, aware it might be someone else trying to pick her up. The packed bar contained lots of men, most in groups of three or more. A lone woman would be considered easy pickings.

The waitress turned, sending her long black ponytail swinging. "Let's see, he's... I dunno, girl. He was right over there, but I don't see him. Looks like he left. Maybe he's in the men's room." With a shake of her head and a swish of her hips, she moved off.

Lea examined the drink. Rum and Coke? Definitely alcohol, possibly laced with something. Whatever it was, she wasn't touching it.

Drink in hand, she continued to scan the crowd.

"Do you think it was him?" Marc asked from beside and slightly behind her. He'd taken a bar stool next to her.

"I hope so," she muttered. "But I don't see him. You know I'd recognize that bastard anywhere."

"He knows that, too. The drink might have been from anyone, you know. I've noticed half a dozen guys eyeing you with interest. It was probably just some guy hitting on you."

Was that jealousy coloring his voice? Nah, most likely he was as tired as she. "Who knows? If it was Feiney, then he knows we're here and that we're playing his game. Just in case, I'll wait."

"And I'll circulate." Marc moved away again, blending back into the crush of people.

A headache blooming behind one eye, she felt that the music seemed louder and more annoying, the air smokier and more difficult to breathe. The longer she sat, pretending to sip her unwanted drink, the harder it was to force a smile.

Though she waited at least twenty minutes and had to brush off three guys, one of them so drunk she had to signal for the bouncer, the guy in the blue shirt never returned to claim his thanks for the drink.

Every instinct told her it had been Feiney.

Later that evening, the headline band took the small stage and began to play. Lea stood and stretched, the headache beginning to throb. Stifling a yawn, she looked around for Marc. She didn't know how much longer she could hold on here.

"Any sign of him?" Marc appeared at her elbow.

"Not a one."

He nodded. "Ready to go?"

"Definitely."

Side by side, not touching, they began making their way through the press of bodies, aiming for the door that led to the parking lot. On the way, a man with a linebacker's build bumped Lea, splashing his drink on her arm. She jumped back, but not quickly enough to keep from getting wet.

Great. Now she smelled like she'd taken a bath in beer.

"There you are," the chubby cowboy slurred. "I've got something for you."

As he began fumbling in his pocket, Marc moved between them and grabbed his arm.

"Easy there," the guy protested, squinting up at Marc. "This don't concern you. I've got somethin' for the lady."

"Are you reaching for a weapon?" Marc's tone sounded stern, using what Lea privately thought of as his law-enforcement voice.

The guy's bloodshot eyes widened. "Jeez, no. That would be illegal. I'm just delivering a message."

Finally, he pulled a slip of paper from his jean pocket. Squinting, he uncrumpled it and then he waved it triumphantly in the air, leaning around Marc to peer at Lea and nearly falling.

"Here you go." He held out the paper.

Marc snatched it as the man tried to pass it to Lea. "Who's this from?"

Weaving slightly, the cowboy turned to squint at the bar. "Guy over there. He's been sitting next to me most of the night. He must have left when I went to the can. Danged if I can find him now."

"What was he wearing?" Lea asked urgently. "Do you remember?"

"Remember? Like I'd forget that." The linebacker snickered. "Dude was wearing a really loud blue shirt. It practically glowed. I'm surprised you didn't see him."

Blue shirt. The same guy who'd sent her a drink. Coincidence? Lea doubted it.

"Go on about your business, now." Marc motioned him away.

Rather than moving, the huge man stood his ground, frowning. "Are you a cop? Cuz you sure sound like a cop."

"Go." At the warning look Marc gave him, the inebriated man shook his head and stumbled away.

"Let me have the note." Lea held out her hand.

Still frowning, Marc passed the paper to her. "Wait until we're in the car."

She dug in her heels. "What if he's still here and wants to meet?"

"He's not."

"You don't know that." Scanning the crowd again, she studied anyone wearing blue. "Though I admit I don't see him."

"He's gone." Though Marc waited with every appearance of patience, the tenseness in his shoulders and the clenched set of his jaw told her it was an act.

Startled, she looked away. When had she become an expert at reading Marc Kenyon?

Slowly, she opened the note.

*Nice outfit* was all it said. The two words were enough to make her want to swear.

"Here." Passing it to Marc, hoping her hand didn't shake, she checked out the crowd once again.

He read the note slowly. "Nice outfit? What the hell does that mean?"

"Feiney just wants to let us know he was here. *Was* being the operative word." She grabbed Marc's arm. "He's not careless, but let's go ahead and make one more thorough check of the room, just in case. He could be disguised."

Beside each other, they moved through the room, inspecting with a casual carefulness each person. Most patrons, busy drinking and socializing, barely noticed them. A few gave them curious looks, a couple of obviously inebriated people grinned, but Marc and Lea saw no one who resembled Feiney.

Finally, when they reached the last table before the door, she turned to Marc, ready to concede defeat.

"You're right. He's gone." The headache had intensified with every step and now the smoky air made her feel ill. "Let's get out of here."

With a tight smile, he nodded. "You don't have to tell me twice."

Once outside, she breathed in big gulps of clear, unpolluted air.

"Are you all right?"

"Yeah." She wiped her mouth with the back of her hand. "I'll feel better the longer I'm out of there."

The ride home went faster now that there was less traffic. Bone weary, Lea stared straight ahead, wishing she could stop being so überconscious of the man beside her. For his part, Marc fell into silence, apparently disinclined to discuss the singular failure of the evening, which faintly bothered her.

Feiney *had* contacted her. She hoped. While the note might have been from some random guy commenting on her clothes, she had to believe it was Feiney.

And that he would contact her again.

Forcing herself to relax into her seat, she thought back over the night. Though she found the entire bar scene repellent, the night had been unsettling in more ways than one. Oddly enough, even more than the note potentially from Feiney, what really disturbed her was the slow dance with Marc.

His kiss had made her curious, but being held in his arms made her hunger. He'd felt rugged and manly and sexy as hell. Her libido, something she'd actually believed had permanently vanished, had come back with a vengeance.

Glancing sideways at him while he drove, she wondered if she affected him the same way. She couldn't stop thinking about how wonderfully solid his muscular body had felt. Desire coiled in her gut, making her want to grab him and kiss him senseless.

As if she'd ever do such a thing. She sighed. Maybe she really did just need to get laid.

The sooner the better.

Finally, they turned into her apartment parking lot. One of the pole lamps was dark, probably from a burned-out bulb.

Walking next to him, she stifled the urge to take Marc's hand. He glanced over at her and, catching her staring, gave her a slow, friendly smile. "Are you all right?"

From somewhere, she found her voice. "I think so." What she wanted to say stuck in her throat. She wanted to invite him to share her bed. Pure foolishness. Yet the thought, once in her head, wouldn't go away.

Climbing the outside stairs, she caught a whiff of herself and grimaced. She hated that she smelled of cigarette smoke and sweat and alcohol. She didn't understand why some women craved being at the bars night after night. Whether they went for the noise or excitement, the music or solely to meet the wrong kind of men, it wasn't her scene. She detested the entire atmosphere, other than the music. Although she liked to dance, she didn't enjoy the crowds of perspiring bodies. Breathing air stale with cigarette smoke and whiskey made her head hurt, and she preferred high heels over Western boots.

Still, she'd do what she had to if it meant catching Feiney. But it seemed he was more interested in stretching out his twisted little game.

As they neared the landing at the top of the stairs, Marc took one look at her face and shook his head. "Hey, at least we accomplished something. Feiney knows we were out there."

"If the note really was from him."

"Oh, it was. I have no doubt."

And he'd recognized her. Of course he'd recognized her. Dangerous, yet necessary.

"It's been too long since he made actual contact," she complained. "This note crap is just a stupid diversion. We haven't heard a peep from him since he captured those girls and dumped the one body."

"I know," he said. "It's slow going right now but we did establish contact, even if it was only a note. I think—Lea, don't move."

The front door of her apartment was propped open.

"Wait here." Marc pushed her to the side and drew his weapon. He kicked the door all the way open. "FBI," he announced.

"I've got your back." Drawing her own gun, Lea motioned him in. Like hell was she going to wait like an unarmed civie while he scoped out her home.

# Chapter 8

The living room appeared untouched. She paused a moment to take stock of her belongings. Flat-screen HD TV, Blu-ray player, Bose stereo—all untouched. It almost appeared as though she'd left her door open by accident, when she knew she'd closed and locked it.

Someone had been in her apartment. She could hazard a guess who. A chill skittered across her skin. If Feiney had been inside, he'd come for a purpose. Now all she had to do was locate the message. She hoped it wasn't anything as gory as the severed hand he'd left in Marc's fridge.

"Feiney?" Marc asked, touching her lightly on the shoulder.

Not willing to trust her tongue to speak, she settled for a nod instead.

"Let's keep looking then." Marc's grim tone told her that he, too, understood.

Keeping the search slow, they methodically checked

everything in the room. Next stop, the kitchen. Like the living room, the kitchen looked the same as always. All the appliances were still in their familiar places.

"Anything missing?" Marc asked, his eyes dark with worry.

"Not so far. It's like we imagined the open door."

"You know we didn't."

"Yes. And you know he never takes anything, only leaves something. I wonder if he arranged for us to be gone," she said.

"I didn't think of that, but I bet you're right. Feiney arranged the false sighting, before knowing we'd head out there."

"Yep. He was making a distraction so he could break into my apartment."

"Now all we need to do is find his little gift. Let's see if it's in here." As he spoke, he pulled open the refrigerator door and peered inside. A moment later, he did the same with the freezer. When he faced her again, he shook his head. "Nothing. I guess that was too much to hope for."

"Yeah. Feiney's nothing if not original. So it's somewhere else."

Dread pooling in the pit of her stomach, she forced herself to take a step and looked around. "We haven't checked the bedroom yet."

Even as she spoke, she couldn't make her feet head in that direction. Partly because she knew in her heart of hearts that's where Feiney would have left his message. In her bedroom, the most personal room in the apartment. Of course.

The familiar frustration began to fill her, making her long to go for a run. She tamped it down, wanting to save her energy now.

"I'll go look." Marc headed down the hall.

"Wait up." No way was he checking without her. After all, the message—whatever it might be—would be meant for her.

"Crap." He stopped short in her doorway and she nearly ran into him.

"Let me see." She shouldered him aside.

As he made room for her to stand beside him, she finally saw Feiney's gift. A huge blow-up doll, wearing Western jeans and boots and a cowboy hat, had been propped up on her bed. The doll, her comforter and pillows were all covered in daisies, with blood trailed like syrup over everything.

"At least it's not another body part," Marc deadpanned.

"Yeah." She walked around the bed, inspecting it from both sides. Again her hatred of Feiney began to flare and this time she allowed it, knowing this would sharpen her mind.

"Whose blood?" she wondered out loud. "I sure as hell hope it doesn't belong to that poor girl."

"The CSI people can figure that out." Cell phone already out, Marc called it in.

The worst part was not knowing. The lab could take weeks getting them the needed results.

"I'll get them to rush this up," Marc said, almost as if he read her mind. "The missing girl's life might depend on that."

"Good. Let's get out of here so we don't disturb the evidence. One wrong footstep and Forensics will be all over us."

They went to the living room to wait. Lea couldn't stop rubbing her arms. She literally felt as though her skin was crawling.

"I swear," she said out loud, "if I could put my hands around Feiney's throat right now..."

She didn't finish the thought. She didn't have to. Marc's expression told her he completely understood.

Later, when the crime-scene technicians had finished, and the CSI team had just about finished peppering her with questions she couldn't answer, her boss Stan showed up.

"Are you ready for that safe house now?" he asked by way of greeting, his expression carefully blank.

Unwilling to let him see the sorrow his words caused, she turned her head and gave him a long, arresting look. "No. There's no need."

"No need?" he repeated. "A crazed serial killer has just broken into your home, left you a gory message of what he intends to do to you and you can't see a need to protect yourself?"

Refusing to let him bait her, she crossed her arms and said nothing.

After a moment, he looked away and shrugged. "You need to understand. I can't guarantee your protection. We're trying like hell to catch this guy, and we'll be watching the place, of course, but still..." He let his words trail off.

Glancing at him again, for the first time ever, she read genuine concern in his brown eyes. He'd come because he was seriously worried. Nothing more, nothing less. She supposed she should be grateful but, in light of everything else, that too pissed her off irrationally.

Breathing deep, she again pushed her roiling emotions under the surface. Attempting a smile would be more than she could muster, but she slung her arm around Stan's narrow shoulders, shocking the hell out of him.

"Don't worry," she said, gesturing at Marc. "I've

got twenty-four-hour protection these days. He'll watch over me."

To his credit, Stan didn't even blink. "Kenyon? What are you talking about? You were serious about you two being, er, friends?"

"Yep. I even let him move in."

Stan's face went beet-red. Jaw tight, he jerked his head in a nod and turned away. Moving to where Marc and the rest of the team were discussing this latest development, he took Marc's arm and motioned him outside, no doubt to lecture him about his responsibilities as a sheriff regarding a special agent who was out on medical leave due to emotional trauma.

This actually made her want to laugh. So much so that she bit the inside of her cheek to keep from cracking a smile. Thanks to Stan, the tension delivered courtesy of Feiney had finally been broken.

She could just make out Stan's steady drone outside and she let herself smile a little. She could imagine what crap her boss would be laying on poor Marc. Hopefully this would break the tension for him, too.

Once he got over his initial shock, she knew Marc would appreciate the jolt back to reality.

Now watching the rest of the team pack their gear and prepare to leave, she checked her bed and saw they'd left the doll. Since there were bloodstains on her linens, the crime-scene guys had bagged her comforter and sheets. But they'd ignored the damn doll, leaving it on the floor on a white paper sheet.

"Excuse me?" She jerked her thumb toward the bedroom. "You're forgetting something."

The technician raised a brow. "What?"

"The blow-up doll. Feiney's present. Aren't you going to take it with you?" she asked, hooking her thumbs in the pockets of her jeans and affecting a bored, indifferent tone, as if she didn't care.

"Nah," Guillermo Romero replied, straight-faced. "We figure Marc might need it on one of his long, lonely nights spent here with you."

She stared back for the space of one heartbeat, then two, before Romero burst out laughing.

"Gotcha," he said, grinning. "As if you didn't know. Of course we're taking it. It's evidence."

She was actually able to grin back. How she missed the easy camaraderie between the guys. Perfect for chasing away the fresh demons brought on by Feiney's reappearance in her life.

Once the last technician vanished out the door, leaving her alone in the apartment, she began to pace. Twice now Feiney had left her a message and both times she didn't get it.

One, a severed hand. Female, jewelry still attached. Two, an inflatable doll, its meaning crude but clear. What she couldn't figure out was how the two went together.

What was Feiney trying to say? Would knowing the answer to this save his poor captive's life? Frustrated, she stopped clenching her fists and summoning up the self-discipline to keep from punching something. When Marc came back inside, they needed to sit down and brainstorm. Maybe between the two of them, they could find the answer to Feiney's riddle.

She resumed her pacing and her cell phone rang. Mid-stride, she froze. Predictably, the ID said Caller Unknown. As she flipped it open, her heartbeat kicked into double-time.

"Feiney," she answered. "I got your little present. Surely you'll understand if I don't say thanks."

"You're all alone for a moment, I see," he purred. "Did

you like my gift? Symbolic, wouldn't you say? You never gave me an answer on the wedding ring."

*Wedding ring? Had the severed hand been merely a method to deliver a ring?* As she pondered this, she realized what else he'd said. *He saw that she was alone?* Once more, her skin began to crawl. Her earlier instincts had been trying to tell her something. "Uh, Feiney? How do you know I'm alone?"

He only chuckled, an answer in its own way.

Cameras? The pyschopath had left cameras? As alarm ricocheted through her, she had to battle to keep her calm demeanor. No way did she want him to know how he affected her.

Okay, so he was watching her. How? Turning slowly, she began to inspect her own apartment, searching for hidden cameras.

"Don't bother looking," he boasted. "You won't find anything. I got an audio and video unit set up. It's well hidden, with a remote feed to me."

Even knowing now she'd have to call back the team and have the Bureau's best electronics gurus sweep her apartment, the knowledge that Feiney was watching her made her ill. She clenched her teeth and swallowed hard, fighting the urge to curse him out.

In this instance, silence was her friend. So she clutched the phone and resumed her pacing.

"Lea, I know you're still there."

"Yep," was all she said, her voice as monotonous as she could make it.

He sighed. "What, no snappy comeback? Talk to me," he ordered. "Did the ring please you? I left your gift in *his* apartment and his gift in yours. They both have special significance, you understand that, right?"

Special significance? Jeez. Even thinking about that tangled mess made her stomach churn.

Feiney continued talking. "Don't you at least want to know whose blood I used?"

Swallowing back the bile that rose in her throat, she shook her head in case he could see. "You know what, Feiney? I'm tired. Your games are boring, especially when the meaning is so obscure that I can't figure it out. From now on if you want to give me presents, give them to me face-to-face."

With that, she disconnected the call. Dropping the cell phone on her end table, she shoved her hands down inside her pockets to hide the fact that her hands were shaking. Since she had no idea where the camera—or cameras— were, she didn't want to take a chance that Feiney would see.

The front door opened and Marc stepped inside. One look at her face and he hurried over.

"What's up?"

Instead of answering, she shook her head. Snatching up her phone, she gestured at him to follow as she headed back toward the door. He came without protest.

Once outside, she closed the apartment door and held up the phone. "Feiney called again. From the way he talked, he has a camera in there. At least one, maybe more. The bastard was watching me."

His expression never changed, though a muscle worked in his jaw. "Son of a—"

"I want the place swept. Do you want to call it in or shall I?"

"Let me do it. You know the Bureau will send a team to check it out." Already reaching for his phone, he dialed, listened and then left a brief voice message.

"They should be calling back shortly, as soon as they get the message. It's after-hours."

"Yeah." The fact that she couldn't seem to stop rubbing her arms irritated her. On top of that, she also couldn't seem to get warm. Physical reactions to psychological stimuli. None of which she wanted or needed. She'd prefer to be detached, robotic and efficient, especially if it helped her get Feiney.

All she wanted out of life right now came down to that.

Marc touched her arm, startling her out of her thoughts.

"What do you want to do?" he asked, his deep voice rolling over her, comforting when she didn't want comfort. Yet in an odd paradox, she wanted to lean into that voice and let it wrap around her like a soothing blanket. She wanted to lay her head against Marc's broad, muscular chest and let him fill her with calmness.

Which meant she was weak. No. Straightening her shoulders instead, she shifted her feet and uneasily glanced back at her front door. "What do I want to do? I have no idea, not right now. All I know is, until the cameras are gone, I'm not staying here. No way do I want that SOB watching me. Can I stay at your place?"

"Sure, assuming he didn't put cameras there, too. We didn't have it checked."

She shuddered.

"Do you want to get a hotel room for tonight?" His dark gaze searched her face. "We can get one, or two if you'd like."

Her heart skipped a beat. Feeling slightly foolish, she nodded. "Two is probably a good idea."

"Do you want to go back in and grab a few things?"

About to say no, she considered. "You know what, I

was going to refuse to set foot in there until they pull that camera, but now..."

"Now you'd sort of like to go in there and give him the finger, right?"

She stared. "How'd you know that?"

"Because I'm feeling the same way."

This actually made her smile. Side by side, they went back into the apartment to pack their bags.

Once in her own bedroom, Lea didn't close the door. Having cameras in unknown locations completely negated the concept of privacy. She packed quickly, half expecting her phone to ring and Feiney to ask her what the hell she thought she was doing, but it didn't.

When she'd finished, she went looking for Marc, who was already waiting in the living room. He stood, lifting his bag. "Are you ready?"

She nodded, unwilling to speak where Feiney could hear, well aware the rawness of her emotions might resonate through her voice.

Once outside, she locked the door behind her.

"When we hear from the electronics people, we'll meet them back here." She started down the stairs at a jog, hating that she felt the need to escape from her own home.

"Hey." Grabbing her arm, Marc stopped her at the bottom of the staircase. "If we're going to stay in a hotel, let's go to Fort Worth. Closer to our target area. Why stay here in Dallas if we don't have to?"

Cowtown. Feiney's hunting grounds and her least favorite place on the planet, because it reminded her of him. The thought made her so angry she could barely speak.

From somewhere, she found her voice. "Why? Why should we make it easier for Feiney? At least if we're here in Dallas he has to drive between the two cities. Unless he's using helpers to do his dirty work."

Gaze locked on hers, Marc reached out slowly and cupped her chin. "Why are you always so angry?"

This close to him, with his steady blue gaze boring into hers, she couldn't seem to summon up even a dose of her rage. Normally, this would have frightened her. But in this very instant, she didn't feel the slightest bit fearful.

"You noticed, huh?"

He nodded.

She thought about her answer, then decided he deserved the truth. "Yes, I'm always angry. It's better than being afraid."

"I understand," he said quietly. Somehow she knew he did. "You're not just angry at Feiney, or at me for letting you get captured. You're furious with yourself."

Inexplicably, her throat clogged and her eyes ached. Instead of trying to speak, she nodded.

"That kind of burden must be difficult to bear."

Her immediate gut reaction was to pop off, say something cutting and smart. But she knew he was only trying to help and, oddly enough, she appreciated that.

Instead, she met his gaze and dipped her chin. "Can we change the subject?"

"Sure. About the hotel—"

"You know what? You're right. Let's stay in Fort Worth. I'm tired of basing my decisions on Feiney."

"Attagirl," he said, though he wasn't smiling.

Shrugging, she tried to push away her sudden exhaustion. "To be honest, I don't really care where we sleep tonight, as long as there's a bed so I can get a good night's sleep. I want to be on my guard even more now. I think our little scenario might work, now that he's contacted me and left me a gift."

"Maybe... I don't know. I think if we want to bring him out, we're using the wrong approach." He glanced at her. "We can challenge him, which is fine, but all that's going to accomplish is make him delight in the game."

"I thought we agreed this would be the best way to draw him out."

He gave her a tight-lipped smile. "That was before your gift and the cameras. The fact that he's going this far, rather than simply attempting to grab you again, tells me that he'll continue to stretch this game out as long as possible, all the while continuing to terrorize women. He's having a blast and doesn't want it to end."

Damn. Though she didn't want to believe it, she knew he was right. "Then what do you suggest we do?"

"I've been thinking about this, and you're not going to like it, but hear me out. You have two choices." He cleared his throat. "One, you've got to pretend to be pining for him. Tell him you've missed him. Reminisce about your time together. Say you feel incomplete without him—"

"Okay, okay. I get it." She felt like she might throw up. Squaring her shoulders, she met his blue gaze. "Marc, you know I'll do whatever I have to do to draw him out in the open and keep another girl from getting hurt, but Feiney's not an idiot. He knows better. What's the other choice?"

"The second option is to make him jealous. Of me."

"What?" She froze. "Explain."

"Feiney views you as his possession. If you act like you're in love with someone else, aka me, eventually he'll grow so infuriated that he'll have to make a move."

Part of her was tempted—oh, so tempted. The other part, the rational, special agent part, was more logical. "That could be dangerous."

He lifted a brow. "How so?"

Unbelievably, she felt her face heat. "To be blunt,

I'm a woman, you're a man. What if things get too…
complicated?"

"Complicated? You mean emotionally?"

"Partly." She swallowed, feeling absurdly foolish. "I was
thinking more about sexually." And she waited for him to
laugh.

He didn't. "I promise things will never go further than
you want them to, Lea. Playacting is playacting. I won't
lose control."

Oh, man. She rubbed the back of her neck. Even
picturing him out of control made her feel hot all over.
Worse, it wasn't him she was worried about. It was
herself.

"Look, if you think it's a bad idea…"

"No." She hastened to reassure him. "I want Feiney
caught and the sooner the better. I'm just not sure I
can…"

"Pretend to be attracted to me?" He sounded rueful.

"That's not it." Face on fire, she dragged her gaze up
to meet his. "I'm going to be blunt. I used to enjoy sex as
much as anyone else. But ever since Feiney, I'm not sure I
can."

His eyes darkened. "Playacting, Lea. It's only playacting.
You can do that, can't you?"

Unable to look away, she swallowed and finally
nodded.

"Glad we're in agreement. But there's more… Not only
do we need to step up the intensity, but I think if there
is more than one camera in your apartment, you should
consider letting the team find all but one. Let that one
stay."

She didn't even have to think about her answer. "No.
Absolutely not."

He held up a hand. "Let me finish. We're having a

team sent here. They sweep, remove all the cameras, but miss one. So we pretend we think they're all gone, that everything's fine and that Feiney can't see or hear us."

Intrigued, she waited.

"We can make plans and Feiney will believe them, only they can be false. We can set a trap that way. We can stage a lot of stuff, really convince him that we're a couple. Infuriate the bastard, goad him into acting."

"Wow." Crossing her arms, she studied him. "Are you serious?"

"Very serious."

The plan sounded so preposterous, so out there that it just might work. She took a deep breath. "All right, we'll try it. Just not in my bedroom, okay? No cameras there or in the bathroom."

He grinned. "Agreed. After the place is swept, all we need to do is convince him that we're a couple."

Though technically she'd already agreed, she was having trouble forming a coherent thought. All she could think about was how strongly his kiss had affected her and how difficult it would be to maintain an objective distance if she was allowed to touch him whenever and wherever she wanted.

"We haven't even heard from anyone yet."

"I know." He dug out his phone. "Let me make another call. I want that team out here ASAP."

"I'm sure they won't be able to get out here tonight," she mused.

Phone already out, he nodded as he dialed. This time, apparently, someone answered. After he told them what he needed and when he needed it, he closed his phone. "They're on the way."

Surprised, she stared. "Now?"

"Yep."

"ETA?"

He shrugged. "Shouldn't be more than half an hour."

"Then I guess there's no need to go to a hotel." Feeling suddenly awkward, she stuck her hands down into her pockets and glanced at her front door. "Now what?"

"How about we go back inside and wait?"

She couldn't stop herself from instinctively recoiling. "I think I'm fine out here."

"Remember, we have a role to play."

"Not yet. Once the team gets here, I'll feel better. Just make sure you explain everything to them."

He beamed at her. "I will."

A little later, a white panel-van pulled into the parking lot. Four men, all wearing black, jumped out and came thundering up the stairs. After greeting Marc and listening to his low-voiced instructions, they all filed into the apartment.

"Come on." Marc took Lea's arm. "I can't let you stay outside. We don't have any idea how close Feiney is."

Reluctantly, she followed him closer to the door. "I need time to get used to the idea of him watching."

He gave her a long look. "No, you don't. Lea, you've got to start thinking of this as an undercover assignment. We need to go in there and put on a show."

He was right. Squaring her shoulders, she tried to think past the horror of her memories, to become her undercover persona. "What do you want to do?"

"I was thinking, I don't know, like maybe I should comfort you. After the team leaves, of course."

Her heart began to thud so loudly in her chest that she wondered if he could hear it. "Are you serious?"

"Completely." Another long look from those dark eyes. "Why? Do you think you can't pull it off? Am I too repugnant to you or something?"

She opened her mouth, then closed it. "I...I don't know what to say."

"Truth between partners," he reminded her.

She took one breath and let it out slowly, then took another. "I don't find you repugnant."

Marc's slow grin not only took her breath away, but made her remember that she'd hinted to Stan that she and Marc were a couple.

"Nor do I find you overly attractive," she said hurriedly, justifying the small lie as a necessary evil to save face.

"Same here," he shot back. "I mean, you're not bad to look at and all, but still..."

Oddly enough, this offended her. Realizing she was never going to understand her own weird, off-the-wall reactions to this man, she decided to go with the flow. "So you're saying *you* wouldn't be able to do it?"

The completely innocent look on his face had to be feigned. The husky sexiness of his voice wasn't.

"Sugar," he drawled, "believe me when I say I can do it. Anytime, anywhere. You just let me know when you're ready."

# Chapter 9

Despite knowing he was joking, Lea's entire body went from hot to cold, then hot again. Damn. Who knew? She had to turn away for a moment to compose herself, afraid she'd laugh—or cry—or worse, challenge him to prove it so she could kiss him again.

Taking a deep breath, she glanced up at him. "When I say *it,*" she clarified in a strangled tone, "I mean the performance for Feiney, not…"

"I get it." He sounded like he was holding back laughter of his own. "I'm *teasing* you, Lea. Trying to break the tension."

Again, conflicting emotions. Both irritated and amused. Finally, she gave in to the humor. "Fine…sorry. I know I'm a little tense. Let's go inside. As you've so carefully reminded me, this is an undercover operation, after all. I can do this."

"Of course you can." He squeezed her hand. "Though

you'd better loosen up a little. We've got to make it look natural."

For the first time since her capture and subsequent release from Feiney's clutches, she tried to summon up her anger and couldn't. For the first time in a long time, the slow and steady burn that had fueled her every move was noticeably absent. She didn't know whether to be alarmed or elated.

"First we've got to establish that there *is* a relationship. This will be the first Feiney's heard of it being more."

"I know. And I'll play to that." He seemed remarkably confident. "I'll be the possessive boyfriend and all that. Think of the heat that will generate."

Did she ever. Closing her eyes, she swallowed hard before opening them.

His grin widened as he leaned in closer to whisper in her ear. "We can fight, then make up. Hot. Passionate. Take that, Feiney."

Oh. My. God. Nose barely inches from his, her heartbeat went crazy. Though she knew this was strictly playacting, undercover, *not real,* she couldn't help but react. Even picturing what he proposed—the making-up part—sent a frisson of heat through her and a delicious shiver up her spine.

"After the team leaves," she reminded him. Her voice sounded strangled, as if she was choking on the words.

He didn't appear to notice. "Exactly. It's important that we convince Feiney that we think all the cameras are gone."

"And I really don't want to go back in there until the team is finished."

"Fine." Leaning back against the brick wall, he crossed his arms. "Lea, why'd you tell Stan that we were together?"

She felt a pang of remorse. "I'm sorry. I was just trying to ruffle Stan's feathers. He was acting way too smug." She took a deep breath. "Now it seems the joke's on me."

"Maybe." Far from angry, he searched her face. "He gave me a long warning about interdepartment affairs and all that."

Suddenly, the joke didn't seem like a good idea after all. "I guess he took me seriously."

He gave her a wry smile. "Sort of."

"If you want, I'll call him and let him know I was only feeding him a line of B.S."

"Not necessary." Something in his tone…

Damn. "What did you tell him?"

Now his smile blossomed into a full-out, butt-kicking grin, taking her breath away. "I told him I'd be gentle."

Stunned speechless, for a second she couldn't move, couldn't think. Eyeing him standing slightly in front of her, silhouetted by the outside light, so big and perfect and beautiful and masculine. They were trying to catch a crazed serial killer, and right this instant all she could think was that she didn't want Marc to be gentle, she wanted hard and rough and furious. Whoa. Better. Stop. Now.

Face flaming, she mustered a smile, aware hers was only a pale imitation of his. "Don't even go there."

"You started it," he quipped. Then, smile slowly vanishing, he gave her a serious look. "Just remember. Don't start something you can't finish."

And there he had it. Playacting aside, this was his way of reminding her that, no matter what, this was only a ruse to catch Feiney. As if he had to. She understood that better than anyone.

"Duly noted." And understood. She'd do well to keep that in mind, especially concerning the burgeoning and completely inappropriate desire she felt for him.

One of the black-clad men stepped outside. "Guys, this is gonna take a lot longer than we expected. So far we've found two hidden video feeds, but there could be more. No audio yet, though."

Lea glanced at Marc, then back at the electronics expert. "How is that possible? We weren't gone that long."

"Who knows? It depends how many people were here doing the installing."

"I seriously thought there was only one camera. The fact that he did more…" She swallowed.

The tech whistled. "He's good. Really good. Honestly, from the scope of this setup, it was done over several hours, at the least. Unless he had a team helping him."

"That's feasible," Marc said. "We don't know who all might be helping him on the outside. Someone has to be."

The tech nodded. "Anyway, we're hard at work removing everything."

"Except one," Marc interrupted.

"Exactly." The guy rubbed the back of his neck. "My point is, this could take all night. If you want to get any sleep at all tonight, you'd better go somewhere else." With that, he turned and went back inside.

Displaced and stunned, Lea waited for the familiar energy of her rage, but it never came. Instead, she found herself wondering what exactly Feiney had witnessed.

Marc was apparently thinking the same thing. "If the bugs and cameras have been there all along…"

"Then he knew everything we planned, even before we did it."

"Exactly." A muscle worked in his jaw. "Except for the little plan we hatched out here on the landing."

"What I don't get is why he tipped me off. I mean, why'd he even bother to tell me he was watching me?"

"The game, Lea. You've got to keep that in mind. He's playing with us because it's all a source of amusement and entertainment. He was probably getting bored and decided to ratchet up things a notch."

Feeling hollow and exhausted, she nodded, missing the comfort of her familiar anger and not sure why she couldn't find it. Maybe in the morning. Assuming she was able to get a good night's rest.

Looking up, she found Marc watching her.

"What do you want to do?" he asked. "Wait for the techs to finish or go find a hotel?"

She didn't even have to think. "Hotel. I don't even care where."

"Come on then. Let's go." He took her arm. Again, she had the nearly overwhelming urge to lean into him, which should have pissed her off but instead only made her feel confused.

Exhaustion. That had to be why. She'd feel more like herself in the morning.

"Let me grab a few things," she said.

Instantly, he agreed. Shoulder to shoulder, they went back inside the apartment.

In the living room, she stopped.

"Are you all right?" he asked.

"No." She shook her head. "I'm not all right. Not only has that SOB broken into my home, but he's invaded my privacy with his stupid cameras."

She turned slowly, her hazel eyes spitting fire as she held out her middle finger. "Feiney, if you're watching, this is for you."

Glancing at Marc, she saw only admiration in his expression. She waited for him to say something.

Instead, he laughed. "I'm sure he's watching or taping. If he doesn't have a microphone in here, he can probably hear us from one in another room. He's probably glued to the monitor because he knows it won't be long before our people locate all his cameras and mikes and take them down."

"True." Lowering her arm, she strolled past him on her way to the bedroom. "The sooner the better."

After she'd tossed a change of clothing into a small gym bag, she met Marc back near the front door, sidestepping busy electronics technicians who were removing her picture frames and inspecting every one of her belongings, from lamps to knickknacks. Trying not to let this bother her, she focused on Marc's steady blue gaze. "Are you ready?"

"I am." He held the door for her. Once it closed behind them, he took her arm.

"By the way," he continued, as they clattered down the stairs. "Change of plan. We're sharing a room. Hold on."

He held up a hand as she started to argue. "Two beds, all right? Two beds. But I'm not letting you out of my sight until Feiney is back behind bars."

Something was wrong with Lea. Putting the car in Drive as he pulled out of the apartment complex parking lot, he glanced over at her, sitting like a silent lump in the passenger seat. He couldn't say for sure why, but she seemed like a shadow of herself, a wraith without impetus. Weird that he even thought in those terms, but there it was.

Maybe after she got some rest, she'd feel better. He could only hope her rapid change of mood was due to apprehension about their upcoming charade. He had to confess, if only to himself, that he was looking forward to it.

She shifted in her seat, drawing his eye. Her delicately carved facial structure and sinful mouth directly contrasted her normal no-nonsense, take-no-prisoners attitude. This at first was what had intrigued him about her, what he thought drew all the guys—the challenge.

But now, having come to know her, he understood it was more than that. Lea Cordasic was broken in ways he couldn't even begin to comprehend. He wanted to help her heal.

As he did nearly every day, he made a silent vow to keep her safe. He couldn't help but remember how, as a child, he'd longed for someone to do the same for him.

Once out on Highway 183, he drove to Loop 820. Glancing again at Lea, he saw that she appeared to have fallen asleep.

He'd stayed at the Suites Hotel in Fort Worth before and that's where he took her now. Once there, he found a parking spot and woke her.

Taking her arm, he led her inside. Still silent, her hair tousled and her eyes sleepy, she looked so unwittingly seductive he wanted to groan.

At the front desk, Marc got a room for one night, using his personal credit card, and asked for two keys. The clerk eyed their lack of luggage with a raised brow, but didn't comment. Which was probably a good thing, as Marc wasn't in the mood for crap. The clerk probably believed they were illicit lovers booking a room for a one-night tryst. Any other time, Marc might have found that amusing. Not tonight.

Their room was at the end of a long hallway. Side by side, they silently walked to it. Lea stood back as Marc inserted his card key, then brushed past him as he held the door open. Holding herself stiffly, she seemed uncomfortable, and the way she avoided looking at him told him she was upset about something.

"Nice room." Her impersonal tone seconded his hunch

that something was up. Wary, he didn't respond, other than with a slow nod. Busying himself with making sure the dead bolt was locked, he put the chain on for good measure before turning around.

"Are you okay?" he asked softly.

She blinked, her smoky hazel eyes meeting his before skittering away. "Just tired." With that, she dropped onto the sofa and nudged off her shoes. Gazing around the room, she leaned back and sighed. "Whew. I'm seriously exhausted."

"Two beds," he said, aware she was only reinforcing her boundaries.

She gave him an impersonal smile, then closed her eyes and let her head loll against the back cushion. Almost as if he wasn't there.

Standing in the doorway, Marc stared at her, aching with more than mere desire. He found her unbelievably beautiful and unbearably sexy. She was made of much sterner stuff than he would have ever guessed.

He wanted her. Unfortunately, he was apparently the only one who felt such desire. Lea appeared determined to keep things on a professional footing, to separate their acting from reality. A lesson he'd do well to remember. If only he could convince his body of that.

He was in danger around her. Danger of losing control, of taking the playacting one step too far. In fact, every time he even thought about the heat they'd generated together, his body instantly responded. He didn't know which was worse—that, or the fact that she appeared to be oblivious to her effect on him.

She made a sound, a slight sigh or yawn, drawing his attention.

"I don't know about you," he said, feigning a yawn, "but

I'm bushed. Wanna catch some shut-eye so we can hit the door running first thing in the morning?"

One of the guys. It was exactly the right tone to take with her. He could tell by the quick glow of relief in her eyes. Rolling her neck, she visibly relaxed.

"Good idea." One corner of her mouth lifted in a half-hearted smile. "You want the bathroom first?"

Telling her to go ahead, he watched her walk away, wondering, once this was all over, if he'd ever see her again.

Waking to the sound of the phone ringing loudly, the first thing Lea realized was that she was pissed. The second, she felt back to normal.

Despite an uncomfortable night trying to sleep while listening to the sound of Marc tossing and turning, she felt rested, rejuvenated and ready to tackle the day.

All that, despite the fact that the bedside clock read 5:00 a.m. and the sun hadn't even risen yet.

In the bed next to hers, a tousle-haired Marc held his cell phone to his ear. As she watched, he grunted a response to something the caller said, then closed the phone.

"That was the all clear," he said, his voice husky from sleep. "We can go home now."

*Home.* For an instant she felt a sharp, swift ache, before she had time to think. Then the familiar and welcome resentment filled her. The all clear meant she'd soon be back in her apartment with Marc, both of them acting like lovers and pretending they didn't know that Feiney was still watching.

Even thinking about that filled her with an odd mixture of fury and—if she was honest with herself—anticipation.

Shaking off the thought, she pushed back the covers

and sprinted for the solo bathroom. "Dibs on the shower," she said, right before closing the door on him.

Later, when both of them had dressed and showered, Lea was about to mention grabbing breakfast somewhere when Marc's stomach growled. Loudly. To her amazement—and probably his—she laughed out loud.

"We'll grab something on the way," he said, correctly interpreting her amusement. "The electronics team is waiting for us at your place."

After a quick stop for breakfast sandwiches and coffee, they arrived at her apartment complex.

A group of three men and one woman stood waiting on the landing outside her door, looking none too happy to still be out at this hour of the morning. Nevertheless, their professional demeanor indicated they'd done exactly what they'd been asked to do.

"How'd it go?" Lea asked softly.

"It took us less than five minutes to find the first camera, the one in the den." The team leader, the same guy who'd told them this job would take all night, dragged his hand through his unruly shock of hair. "The rest were not so easy. That place had more cameras—and remote listening devices—than twenty first-rate interrogation rooms. Your perp placed cameras in the hall, in both bathrooms, in the master bedroom and guest bedroom, as well as one in the entrance."

"You removed all those?"

"Yes."

Marc followed the team down the stairs to the parking lot. "What about the other one, the one you left? Where is it?"

"In the kitchen." The guy rolled his eyes. "Mounted inside that vase on top of the refrigerator. Whoever's monitoring it has a partial view of the den and dining area."

Lea winced. "Ouch."

"Yeah, but that one seemed like it was the least invasive, you know? And since you wanted me to leave one…"

"You did perfect. Thanks, man." Marc clasped him on the arm. "I appreciate it."

Though he nodded at Marc, the team leader looked at Lea. They didn't know each other personally, but they both worked for the Bureau and so shared a peculiar sort of camaraderie.

"Thank you." She held out her hand. "I really appreciate this."

"No problem." Giving her hand a quick squeeze, he dipped his chin, motioned to the rest of his team and they got back in the van and drove off.

"Come on." Lea started for the stairs, relieved when Marc followed without comment. All she could think of was the camera in the kitchen and the act Marc wanted them to put on for Feiney's benefit.

But halfway there, right before they reached the large light pole, she grabbed his arm. "Get down."

He obeyed without question, dropping to the ground next to her and pulling his weapon. "What did you see?"

"Someone over there." Rising to a half crouch, she had her weapon out, too, as she darted sideways next to a large pickup truck, using it as cover. Heart pounding, she glanced back at him. "I heard a scream. It might be nothing."

"But we can't take a chance." This time he lunged forward, letting the large concrete base of the light pole shield him.

A moment later, someone screamed again.

Exchanging a glance with Marc, Lea took off at a run with him right behind her. Still using parked cars to shield them, they went in the direction of the sound, hoping and praying that Feiney hadn't grabbed someone else so close to Lea's home.

The scream came again. A woman—a teenager, actually—ran around the corner, skidding to a stop when she saw them. Close on her heels was a teenage boy. His goofy, besotted grin vanished the instant he saw them and their guns.

Instantly, Lea lowered hers. A second later, Marc did the same.

"Did you scream?" Lea asked, her voice stern though her heart still thudded hard in her chest.

When neither kid answered immediately, she repeated the question, making her tone hard, the law-enforcement voice, demanding an answer.

Sulky, the girl nodded, her long brown ponytail swinging. "We were just playin'."

The boy still hadn't taken his eyes from their weapons. Despite his tough-guy appearance, Lea thought it might be the first time the kid had seen a Glock.

Exchanging a look with Marc, Lea holstered her gun. "Come on." Marc did the same.

He held out his hand. "Let's go."

After a moment's hesitation, she took it, glancing over her shoulder as the kids ran off.

"Better safe than sorry," she said, sounding aggravated and relieved at the same time. "With all this craziness from Feiney, you never know."

"True." He squeezed her hand, reminding her of what lay ahead.

To distract herself, she focused on thoughts of Feiney, successfully bringing back the edges of her antagonism, enough to give her the energy to keep moving forward. "What's frustrating is we keep expecting him to do something. Meanwhile, he's holed up, torturing that poor girl and messing with us."

"True. But maybe once he witnesses our little act of devotion, he'll make a move."

And to that, she had nothing to say at all. With every fiber of her being, she forced herself to concentrate on what she had to do next and believing she'd find a way to remain in control.

His grin widened. "If we hurry." He squeezed her hand, reminding her that their fingers were still linked and making her break into a light sweat. "Ready?"

Feeling anything but, she nodded.

"Lea?" Stopping, he made her look at him. "It's going to be all right. We're going to get this bastard."

"I have no doubt." To her amazement, she realized she actually believed it. Amazing. Was it because she had so much faith in Marc, or because she was learning to have faith in herself again? She didn't have time to ponder the question. For now, they had a show to put on and a lure to cast.

Together, they turned back toward her apartment. As he reached out for the doorknob, she stopped and looked up at him.

"I just want you to know that I…"

"Shh." He smiled as he said it, though his blue eyes had darkened. "Remember, whatever it takes."

He was right. Of course. Still, she worried. Not about performing in front of a monster—no longer that, since Marc was right and she *would* do whatever it took to catch Feiney.

Mostly, she worried simply that in the middle of pretending to make out with Marc, she'd forget she was playacting. That she'd find she enjoyed kissing him way too much.

One final squeeze of her hand for reassurance and they started forward.

# Chapter 10

Once inside, Marc carefully closed the door behind him. He knew that in order to make this believable, he'd have to take the lead.

"I can't believe we had to stay somewhere else last night. I'm sure glad your job gave us quick access to those electronics folks."

Lea grimaced. "Do you think they got them all?" she asked, letting go of his hand and dropping down onto the couch. With a sigh, she leaned back and closed her eyes.

"Yes." Which they both knew was a lie. But they wanted Feiney—if he was listening—to think they believed no one could see or hear them. That they were acting naturally. Two people in love.

For one of them at least, this much was true.

Heart thumping way too fast, he sat down next to her, put his arm around her shoulders and pulled her close. Nuzzling her on the neck, he breathed in her peach-scented skin and tried not to think about how easily he could get used to this. Loving the way she shivered, he nibbled at her earlobe before murmuring. "Play along, sugar."

For only an instant, she went rigid, then relaxed into his arms. "Can he see us here?" she whispered, turning the tables on him by using her tongue to caress his ear.

Now it was his turn to shiver. "I think so," he managed to say, hoping she took the faint hitch in his voice for part of the game.

"Good," she purred, then whispered again. "Play along, pumpkin."

The sarcasm in her fake endearment should have been warning enough. Instead, he let his libido lead him.

With an easy grin for the camera, he pulled her close for a long, body-to-body hug. "Maybe we can—"

"No." Sharp-voiced, she cut him off. "Not now."

Still, her words barely registered. After all, she'd said to play along.

"Why not?" He nuzzled her neck. "We can make it a quick—"

"Marc." This time she shoved him away, hard enough to send him back against the cushions. "I'm not in the mood. Feiney was here, in my home. He left a damn blow-up doll, for Pete's sake. Crime Scene took my new comforter, my sheets and there's still blood on my carpet. On top of that, he had cameras. Cameras." She shook her head furiously. "So don't even think about having sex."

Stunned and feeling like a heel, he stared at her. To his surprise, there were tears in her beautiful, smoky eyes. Talk about getting into character. Which was why she was so good at undercover work—she used the truth to build to a lie. This was more than a masquerade. Underneath her veneer of self-assurance, unfortunately, this was all too real.

"Babe, I'm sorry." Reaching for her again, he noted how easily she evaded him.

She cast him a look of disdain. "Whatever. How about you sleep in the guest bedroom tonight. I don't really want to be around you right now."

Setting parameters. Of course, despite the need to put on a show of sorts, they wouldn't be sharing a bed. Though he honestly regretted this, he also admired the adroit way she accomplished her establishment of the fact.

Playing along, he stood, too, and crossed his arms. "Come on. You can't blame me because Feiney's an ass."

"Can't I?" Her voice would have cut through steel. "You're my boyfriend. A monster has just invaded my private space and all you can think about is a quickie? I'd think you'd have a little more compassion."

He gave her a completely uncomprehending look, as if he didn't get it. "I've got plenty of compassion. Let me kiss and make it up to you. I guarantee I can make you forget about Feiney."

Turning the knife. Good. He hoped to hell that Feiney was watching and listening.

Acting completely offended and shaking her head, Lea turned her back to him and began moving away.

Giving in to temptation, he caught her by the waist as she moved past, pulling her close and planting a hard kiss on her mouth. It felt good enough to stun him.

"Marc…" she warned, rearing back, her eyes wide and full of warning and something more, something darker.

Ignoring this, he pulled her close again.

"I've got my own way of shooting Feiney the bird," he murmured against her mouth. "Let me kiss you one more time."

She wanted to, he could tell. Letting her eyes drift half-closed, still she hesitated. He saw the moment she came to a decision. Whether for the role they played or for herself, with a slight hitch in her breath she lifted her face to his.

Their lips touched. Slowly, reining in his hunger and his impatience, he let himself explore her mouth. Tasting, savoring, claiming.

Though the kiss may have started out as staged, for him it rapidly went beyond that, morphing from a slow, simmering burn into an all-out, raging inferno. More than an act, more than even mere physical attraction, as corny as it seemed to even think it, he felt as if his soul merged with hers.

Christ, what was it about this woman?

Crushing her to him, he knew he couldn't seem to get close enough. Pretend be damned, he knew, too, though dimly, that such a thing would be way beyond the scope of this bit of undercover work.

His body didn't seem to care. Though he fought the urge to grind himself against her, as a man he definitely had other ideas. Such as burying himself deep inside her and pounding into her until they both could think of nothing else.

No, no. Not possible. Instead, he allowed his hands free rein, stroking the creamy softness of her skin, exploring the intriguing hollows of her shoulders, her neck, down the curve of her hip. She quivered, moving against him—or was that away?

Through a haze of lust, he tried to decide.

"Lea?"

"Don't…" she said. Her broken voice tore at his heart, bringing him back to his senses like a dash of ice water in the face.

Instantly, he pulled back. But when he began to move away from her, she gripped his arms.

His pulse leaped when she leaned in close, only to whisper in his ear, "Let's not overdo it here."

Apparently, she still was in full possession of her senses.

Calling himself seven kinds of fool, he grimaced.

"Sorry." Shuttering his expression, he remembered the camera, Feiney, the game…everything. None of it was real. None of it. Unfortunately, his full arousal refused to immediately subside. He still wanted her.

Ashamed and alarmed, he tried to move away.

"Wait." She clutched at him, her huge hazel eyes full of desire. "Don't go yet."

Was she still acting for the camera? She had to be, though the contradictory nature of her words made him want to throw caution to the winds and do what he really wanted.

Ultimately though, he knew she was a professional. As he was. Or, he amended, as he would be, as soon as he got a grip on his raging libido.

He forced himself to remember the role. It was all about the part. Therefore he needed to stay in character. Feiney was watching. A reaction, a little more impetus was needed.

"Never mind," she said.

"Make up your mind," he snarled. "I'm tired of your little games."

Her eyes widened and he saw her tamp down the beginning of a smile. Instead, raising her head, she narrowed her eyes and then sneered at him.

Damn, she was good.

"Who do you think you are?" Yanking her against him, he took her mouth with his. No gentleness here. This time, he ravished her mouth, determined to make her want him as badly as he ached for her. Though he started out in character, only meaning to show her...what? At the first touch of her lips, all rational thought fled. Heat flared between them, searing him, branding them. Damn it all to hell.

He groaned her name. "Lea."

She murmured something back, not his name, not a *no* or a *stop,* but something wordless that sounded like encouragement.

That was all he needed to send his rapidly shredding resolve out the window. Heart hammering in his ears, he pressed his fully aroused body against her, making her gasp.

He had to stop this. Now.

Luckily for him, or for both of them, someone called his cell phone.

Immediately she drew back, her pupils huge and dark, dilated with what he hoped was passion. "You'd better get that."

He couldn't make himself move.

To his disbelief, she leaned in again. Licking delicately at his ear in a way that sent shivers down his spine, she whispered again. "Remember, he's watching."

Hell, was she *enjoying* torturing him? "Lea, I..."

"Get the phone." She laughed. Her amusement was completely convincing. Too convincing. For the first time he realized this might not be as simple as he'd expected.

Slowly, he fished his phone out of his pocket, watching as Lea walked away. She went down the hall, into the bathroom and closed the door behind her with a loud click.

Seeing her too-bright eyes and flushed complexion in the mirror, Lea splashed cool water on her cheeks. Through the closed door, she could hear Marc talking to whoever had called him, his tone telling her it wasn't Feiney.

She shook her head, still dazed. Of course it wasn't Feiney. That sick bastard only called her, not Marc.

She let the anger fill her, needing it to chase away the desire. For no reason at all, she grabbed her toothbrush, squirted on fresh mint toothpaste and began to brush her teeth. Midway through, it occurred to her to wonder if she was trying to scrub away Marc's kisses. As if she ever could forget them.

Even thinking about how he'd possessed her mouth made warmth blossom through her. No man had ever made her feel weak-kneed from just a kiss. Ever. Until now.

Her ire, normally so reliable, fizzled and vanished. Staring at herself in the mirror, she felt like a stranger, all achy and empty in a way she'd never felt before.

She wanted Marc, she *needed* Marc. Touching her intimately. Moving inside of her.

For the first time in ages, she felt alive. Feminine. Looking at her blushing cheeks and radiant eyes, she might even dare to say beautiful. Yes. She felt frickin' beautiful.

Take that, Feiney.

And as she thought of her nemesis, her hatred returned. Tempered this time with regret. None of this was real. When Feiney was captured and sent back to his hellhole in prison, she and Marc would go their separate ways.

She needed to remember that they were just pretending. Though she knew that before all this was over she and Marc might end up having sex—how could they not, when they generated so much heat—she couldn't allow herself to become personally involved. Not now, when her emotions were so delicate and fragile that she herself didn't even trust them. One wrong move and she just might shatter.

She made a face at herself in the mirror. All she could afford to focus on was making sure Feiney was caught. Everything else would have to be secondary. End of story.

Resolve strengthened, she rinsed out her mouth, dragged a brush through her hair and turned to rejoin Marc.

Cell phone to his ear, he looked up when she entered the room. The bleakness in his gaze made her blood turn cold. Dread coiled in her stomach. Something bad had happened. Marc's hunched shoulders and tense neck told her that the caller wasn't giving him good news.

And she'd just bet the call somehow involved Feiney. Everything did, these days.

He muttered something too low for her to hear and closed his phone, shoving it into his pocket.

"What happened?" she asked.

Shaking his head, he met her gaze. "That was one of the team. Feiney did it. He killed the other girl. The FBI is already on-site."

Despite herself, she gasped. "He gave us no warning."

"Does he ever?" Yanking his car keys out of his pants' pocket, he tossed them from hand to hand. "He dumped the body at the back door of Billy Bob's. Same M.O.—cowboy hat and daisies. And blood. Can't forget the blood."

Swearing, she strode to the window so that if he was watching Feiney could see her on that blasted camera of his. "He gave up his leverage."

"For now," Marc agreed. "At least until he grabs the next one. My office and the rest of the team are en route. I'm meeting them there. Want to join me?"

Startled, she nodded, her heart doing double-time. Not wanting to give Marc a chance to remember that she was on medical leave and therefore not authorized to tag along, she hurried out the door after him.

Only once they were in the car, heading toward the Stockyards, did she turn to him and let go of the feeling about to explode inside her.

"We caused this," she said, aware her desperate regret sounded in her voice. "This is Feiney's revenge—the killing. We did this to that girl, us and our little performance in front of his camera."

Immediately, Marc shook his head. "No, Lea. We did not." His tone was firm and certain. She found herself taking a large measure of comfort from that.

Still, she had to ask. "How do you know?"

"Because the body was found as we were just getting warmed up. Feiney killed this girl before you and I even kissed."

The tightness in her chest loosened. "You're right," she breathed.

"It's not your fault, nor mine. Nothing that insane prick does is your fault, do you understand?"

He sounded angry enough for both of them, enough that she could put any lingering doubts to rest.

"We need to focus on our goal," he persisted. "We can't let anything distract us."

Was he talking to her or to himself? Letting her gaze roam over his rugged profile, she sighed. She couldn't help but marvel at how easily he seemed to be able to go from passionate lover to distant law-enforcement professional.

Marc Kenyon was a damn good actor, she'd give him that. Only he hadn't been acting about one thing—his arousal had been real. She certainly hadn't imagined that. Nor would she be able to easily forget it.

"Aren't you going to have a problem with the team when I show up with you? If Stan's there, I can only imagine his reaction."

Jaw rigid, intent on his driving, he barely spared her a

glance. "Not at all. Since Feiney left such a clear message, I already told Stan that I'm not letting you out of my sight."

So help her, her heart skipped a beat. "Clear message?" She swallowed. "What message? Did you forget to tell me something?"

Now he did glance at her, the tight set of his mouth telling her transparently that his omission had been deliberate. "Stan said it's a pretty graphic…er, picture. Visual, more than words. I think you'll need to see it."

*Damn Feiney.* "If it's visual, that means it's not specific. How does Stan know it's directed at me? It could be a message for the media or anyone in law enforcement."

"True, but Feiney wrote your name. In blood. He incorporated that into the display."

Dread coiled low in her belly. "Display. You said this was the same M.O.—daisies, cowboy hat, the usual. What else?"

A muscle worked in his jaw. She could see him debating how to tell her.

"That bad, huh?" she asked dryly. "You might as well tell me now, since I'm going to see it for myself."

"The victim is missing her hand, for starters."

Lea swore. "That sorry sack of—"

"Yeah."

"Who…" Clearing her throat, Lea tried again. "Who was she?"

"Lorna Placek, age twenty-seven. Married, with two small children. She'd gone out with her twin sister to celebrate a promotion at work."

"Her twin sister was the other victim?"

"Unfortunately, yes." With a tired shrug, he returned his full attention to the road. "Yet another reason why I'm not letting you out of my sight."

"Don't get too comfortable in the role of protector," she warned him. "I can take care of myself. Like all the rest of it, this is part of the game to catch Feiney."

He shot her a quick look. "As if I'd ever forget."

Was that a tinge of bitterness in his voice? Surely not. But just in case, she decided she'd better shut up and let him drive.

When they finally arrived at the crime scene, the local police had already roped off the area with yellow tape. Marked and unmarked vehicles surrounded the scene, and uniformed officers stood guard.

Marc parked. Gravel crunching underfoot, they got out of the car. He took her arm and escorted her to the perimeter, where he flashed his ID.

"She's with me," he told the cop.

Her first hint of what was to come—and really, she should have steeled herself to expect it—was the trail of bloody daisies. Her second was the scent. The awful aroma of fresh blood and flowers. The aroma of...Feiney.

Bile rose up inside her throat. She swallowed, hardening her resolve, knowing what Feiney had done to the body, to the girl, wouldn't be pretty. Hell, pretty? It wouldn't be human.

And the daisies—the damn flowers were everywhere. Barely suppressing a shudder, she kicked aside petal after petal. She didn't realize, until Marc placed his hand on her shoulder, that her kicks were growing more and more violent, more and more out of control.

"Are you okay?" His gaze searched her face. "Don't lose it, sugar. Take a deep breath."

After a moment's hesitation, she did exactly that. One deep, calming breath, then another. Finally, she nodded. "I'm fine. Or, I will be," she said grimly. "Lead the way."

Keeping his grip on her arm, he studied her. Whatever he saw in her eyes seemed to satisfy him. As he turned around to continue forward, Stan appeared, waving at Marc. He took one look at Lea and the welcoming expression on his face turned to irritation.

"Kenyon," he barked. "What do you think you're doing?"

"She needed to be here." Marc's calm tone belied his death grip on her arm. "I told you I wasn't letting her out of my sight."

"She's on medical leave." Stan cursed. "My ass will be in a sling if my superiors learn she was out here."

"So we make sure they don't find out."

Stan tried another tack. "What if she can't handle this? She could have a complete breakdown."

"Oh, for Pete's sake." Lea had had enough. "Will the two of you quit talking like I'm not here? I'm not fragile, Stan. I can handle seeing this. It used to be my job, remember."

"'Used to be' are the key words here." Suddenly, Stan's annoyance seemed to fade into weary resignation. "Go away, Lea. This investigation is ongoing. You know as well as I do—as do you, Kenyon—that bringing her here was a mistake."

Expression impassive, Marc indicated the crowd of both medical and law-enforcement personnel blocking them from seeing the crime scene. "You said Feiney left her a message. I think it's important that she see it."

"*You* think?" Stan poked his finger at Marc's chest. "Last time I checked, I was the SAC here. Take her home, Kenyon. Now."

"You're being unreasonable. Marc's part of the team," Lea protested. "He at least has a right to see the victim."

"Not with you here." Stan crossed his arms. "I'm not budging on this one. I could lose my job."

She exchanged a quick look with Marc. "And more women could lose their lives if Feiney's not caught."

Marc's expression told her she'd said too much.

Stan narrowed his eyes. "Since you're not on the team and have no part in the investigation, I don't think whether or not you see the crime scene has any bearing whatsoever on the case."

Squeezing her arm, Marc seemed to be telling her to back down.

"Fine. I'll wait in the car," she conceded. "That way Marc and the rest of you can do your jobs."

"No." Marc's tone sounded as inflexible as Stan's. "I'm not leaving you alone. Not even here. Especially not here."

"Take her home."

Slowly, Marc shook his head. "I work for the sheriff's office, not for you." Still gripping Lea, he began to move forward. "She's coming with me. Come on, Lea. Let's go."

Lea's first reaction was to dig in her heels. Her second—as she caught sight of the fury mingled with relief on Stan's face—was, *what the hell*. They'd already placed her on involuntary medical leave. What else could they do…fire her?

More than anyone on the face of this earth, she had a right to see Feiney's message. After all, he'd left it for her.

Blocking their way, finally Stan jerked his chin in a nod and stepped aside. "Go. But make it quick. The crime-scene people just finished taking photographs. Be careful where you step."

As if he needed to warn them against contaminating the evidence.

Shaking her head, Lea went with Marc to view Feiney's handiwork.

# Chapter 11

The body had been arranged like all the others she'd seen from before Feiney's arrest, trial and subsequent incarceration. Partially clothed, cowboy hat over the face and covered in bloody daisies.

With one major difference. This victim was missing her hand.

He'd wrapped her bloody stump with towels, apparently able to stop the bleeding long enough to keep her alive and in pain. The better to abuse her and kill her at his own convenience. Lea couldn't help but imagine the torturous agony this poor girl had gone through. In terror, she'd most likely begged for mercy, only to be met by this...death and degradation.

Fury—back again, to her relief—filled her so strongly she had to clench her teeth. "I'm gonna get that son of a—"

"Look." Cutting off her words, Marc turned her away from the victim. "The message."

She blinked, at first seeing only flowers and blood. Then, she looked again and saw.

Written in a thin trail of blood, linked by daisies, Feiney had painstakingly left her a message.

*I sent you the ring, Lea. I'm waiting for your answer. You have three more days. Then it's your last rodeo, sweetheart.*

Lea's blood turned to ice. "What does he mean?" Though she already knew.

"The severed hand had a ring. A wedding ring."

Horrified, she swallowed. "You seriously think…"

"That he used this poor victim's ring to propose to you? I wouldn't have thought it, until I saw this message. Who does that?"

His rhetorical question didn't need an answer. They both knew who did that. A madman. Feiney.

"He's given me a time line," she muttered. "Why?"

"I don't know. But I have no doubt he means it. We have three days."

"Then he'll kill again." She blanched. "We've got to stop him."

"Until he contacts you, we need to go back to the apartment and ramp things up. We've got to make him come to us well in advance of the three days."

She swallowed. Further proof that to Marc, all this was a job. That he could stand here and talk about pretending to make out, with the scent of death filling their nostrils…

Apparently, he correctly interpreted her expression, because he leaned in close. "We've got to catch this bastard. Nothing else matters, Lea. Remember that."

He was right. "As if I could ever forget."

One of the crime-scene techs called Marc's name.

"Wait here." Shooting her a quick look of warning, Marc strode away.

The instant Marc bent his head to confer with the forensic specialist and the technician, Stan appeared. "Quit messing with him," he told Lea.

Startled, she eyed him. "I'm not clear on your meaning."

"Kenyon. Quit messing with him. You're not ready and I think he's taking it more seriously than he is letting on."

"I doubt that," she said, realizing he still thought she and Marc were an item. Since she couldn't tell Stan their plan, all she could do was continue to play along. "Since when do you get involved in your employees' personal lives?"

"Hey, look. I might seem like a hard-ass, but I care about all my employees, including you."

"I know you do," she admitted. In his own way, Stan truly cared. "But believe me, I'm not going to get hurt."

"It's not you that I'm worried about. It's him."

"What?" Eyeing Stan, she wondered if he'd finally lost it.

"I like Kenyon. He and I have worked together on several cases and he's a good guy. To you, he's just a random fling. But I get the feeling that with him, it's more than that."

Suppressing the warmth that flooded her at the comment, Lea only smiled. "You have no idea what you're talking about."

"But—"

"You'll understand some day." Cryptic, but as close to the truth as she could skate with her boss, special agent in charge of the Feiney case.

Stan's characteristic arrogance reared its ugly head. "I order you to stop seeing him."

"You *order* me?" She couldn't help but laugh out loud. "Since Marc and I are living together and he's hell-bent to protect me from Feiney's clutches, I couldn't stop seeing him even if I wanted to."

Glowering at her, Stan leaned in. "I swear to you, Cordasic, if you break him, there'll be hell to pay."

She held up a hand. "There's no way to put this nicely, so I'll just say it. Butt out of my personal life."

A muscle worked in his jaw. "Fine. Have it your way. But I want to go on the record as putting you on notice. If you take down one of my best contacts in the sheriff's office, you may not be coming back to work at all. *Capiche?*"

Now his true colors were showing. Had she actually thought Stan gave a rat's ass about her?

"Threats, Stan?" She made a *tsk*-ing sound. "How unprofessional. Also, just so we're clear, what Marc Kenyon does is completely up to him. I don't have anything to do with his decisions."

"Oh, I think you do." Stan glanced over at the crime scene, where Marc was still talking to the CSI guy. "More than you know."

Since his statement made no sense, she didn't bother to comment.

A moment later Marc detached himself from the others and came over. Barely sparing a look at Stan, he took Lea's arm and steered her away. "Come on."

"Be careful, Cordasic," Stan called after her. "You too, Kenyon."

Lea had to bite her lip to keep from snapping off a smart-ass comment.

When they reached the car, Marc glanced at her. "What was that all about?"

"Stan warned me off a relationship with you. He seems to think being with me will mess you up." Though she tossed off the remark casually, Stan's comments still stung.

"Are you serious?" Marc's obvious amusement went far to banish any lingering doubts. "He really said that?"

"Yeah." She gave him a rueful smile. "He called you his best contact in the sheriff's office. I think he's worried that if you and I break up, you'll hate the Bureau."

"That doesn't make sense." Unlocking the car, he opened her door for her, waiting while she got in and made herself comfortable before closing it. "Unless…" he muttered as he climbed in behind the wheel.

"Unless what?"

"Unless Stan's figured out what we're trying to do and that's his way of protesting."

She thought for a moment. "Not Stan. If he'd any idea what we're up to, he'd have brought both guns to bear on us immediately. He's obnoxious that way."

Though Marc nodded, she could tell from his expression that he didn't believe her.

She waited until he'd buckled himself in before asking, "What'd you find out talking to the crime-scene tech?"

He glanced at her with a halfhearted smile as he turned the key in the ignition. "Same old, same old. Whoever did this arranged the body the same way, right down to the daisies and cowboy hat. They're hoping to have a DNA match within a few days."

She picked up on his choice of words. "Whoever did this? Anyone with half a brain knows who did this. Does the CSI guy honestly think it's a copycat?"

"No, but until there's a DNA match, he can't say with a hundred percent certainty. You know that."

She did, though it irritated her. One basic truth of law enforcement was never to assume anything. Still, this case was unique. Two girls vanished, one killed and then, a few days later, the second killed and left in the exact same manner.

Along with the crowning proof—a message written in blood, directed at her.

Taking a deep breath, she nodded. "What was different?" She knew there had to be subtle differences for the copycat assumption to be made at all.

"The placement of the body, for one. The vic's hands weren't placed in the praying position."

"That's because she was missing one!" She frowned. "Is that the only difference? That's not odd enough to assume this must have been a copycat."

"The M.E. says this one wasn't raped."

"Damn." Now *that* was significant. Feiney enjoyed forcing sexual advances on his hapless victims. "I wonder why not."

"Maybe because of the marriage proposal. In his own twisted way, Feiney was trying to honor you."

She nearly gagged. Though it made sense, the thought made her want to puke.

"Lea?" He touched her shoulder, startling her. "You did well back there."

She could have reacted in several ways. Once she might have responded with resentment or indignation. Now, knowing Marc, she took his words as he meant them, as a compliment.

"Thanks. I swear, we've got to get him before he captures any more women. No one should have to suffer like that." Amazing how much more clearheaded she felt when she didn't allow wrath to consume her.

Marc parked the car. Somehow, without her noticing, they'd arrived back at her apartment. Cutting the engine, he pocketed the keys and turned to her. "That's why we've got to step this up. By now, Feiney's probably watched the earlier tape. He's most likely royally pissed."

She regarded Marc hopefully. "Do you think he's mad enough to make a move?"

"I don't know. But we've got to continue to play the game until he contacts you. We can play this two ways— you can pretend to be upset over the crime scene we just saw and I can comfort you, or…"

She raised a brow. "Or what?"

"I don't know. Stage fight. Kiss and make up." He gave her a slow, lazy smile. "Your call."

Something intense flared between them. This time, she knew she hadn't imagined it. With her heart quickening in her throat, it was a moment before she could actually speak. "I vote we play it by ear."

"Done." He got out of the car. Crossing to her side, he opened her door and helped her out, keeping hold of her arm. "Just act naturally," he said.

If he only knew, she thought dryly. He waited while she fit her key in the lock. Together, they entered the apartment.

Marc knew that Lea had no idea of his desire for her. Merely anticipating what they were about to "pretend" to do had his body fully aroused. The strength of his excitement made walking awkward, but walk he did. They made it inside the apartment and he waited while she closed the door behind them, locking both the regular lock and the dead bolt.

Feiney's camera would have a clear shot of them where they stood. When she turned to face him, he pulled her into his arms. "Let me touch you."

A small hitch of breath was her only answer, so he pulled her closer, luxuriating in the feel of her soft, lush body in his arms. He kept himself perfectly still, letting her feel the full strength of his body against her. She couldn't help but realize his arousal now and he waited to see her reaction.

To his surprise, she didn't move. But then again she probably viewed this as just a job that must be done to catch Feiney. The way he was supposed to think of it, but couldn't.

He wanted her too damn badly.

"Touch me," she murmured, face against his chest. "Erase the memory of that bastard from my mind."

At this, he nearly froze. Was this truth or only her method of getting into the role?

Uncertain, he made himself go slowly. Hell, if he wanted to maintain some semblance of control, he had no choice. Trailing his hand up her arm, he marveled at the creamy softness of her skin reflected in the glow from the outside light.

"You're absolutely beautiful, you know. "

"Hmm." She gave him a slow smile full of heat and promise. "So are you."

A wave of desire slammed into him, so strong he couldn't breathe. More than anything, he wanted her passion to be genuine, real. He hadn't expected this, though he should have.

Then, miracle of miracles, she touched him, stroked her fingers across his biceps, catching on his shoulder, before she wound her hand in the thickness of his hair.

"What are you doing?" It came out a growl. "Careful. I'm close to losing control."

Her eyes widened, but instead of moving away, she lightly pressed her lips against his neck. "You?" A teasing note in her voice, she wiggled against him. Sweet torment. "I can't picture you out of control."

He took a great, shuddering breath, frozen in place.

Using her teeth, she lightly nipped his earlobe. "You'd

better get with the program and at least try to act like you're enjoying this," she whispered fiercely in his ear.

Get with the program? Christ, she didn't have the faintest idea how she affected him. Or was she still messing with him? She had to feel his massive arousal, had to realize that, game aside, he wanted her with an aching intensity that bordered on pain.

He needed her to want him the same way.

Two could play this game.

Forcing a carefree smile, he moved away. "I don't know about you, but I'm beat. Let's get something to eat and call it a night."

Surely she had to realize the wrongness of this. Like any red-blooded guy would abandon her sensuous arms for the lure of food.

But Lea, sweet beautiful Lea, bit her lip and eyed him, apparently believing him. Now a faint tinge of pink colored her skin. "Oh." Did she honestly have to sound so...disappointed? "I understand."

"No, you don't." Then, while she tried to contemplate, he knew he had to give her the truth and hope she recognized it for what it was.

"I want you, sugar. If we continue to do this—" Grabbing her, he claimed her mouth for a brief, hard kiss, barely able to pull himself away. "I don't know that I can keep from taking you."

"Taking me?" she repeated, as though she'd never heard the phrase before.

"Yes. Taking you. Deep and hard and fast. I want to bury myself inside you and make love to you until you scream my name."

There. She'd said she wanted only honesty between them. Little did she know he wasn't acting now. Camera be damned, he couldn't seem to control himself with her.

Her flushed face and heightened breathing told him how his words affected her. Her full breasts with high, pebbled nipples practically begged for his touch.

What the hell. He decided to press his point. "You want me, too, don't you?"

Parting her lips, she tried to form a coherent and honest answer. Her eyes told him she did want him, but not here, not now, not in front of Feiney.

Playacting could only go so far.

He waited for her to tell him to go to hell. Instead she shook her head, tossing her hair the way a skittish filly flipped her mane. "I don't know...I don't know what I want."

He did. He wanted the exact same thing. If only it was another time, another place.

Gently, softly, the way one might tend to a wounded bird, he pressed his lips to her cheek, using every ounce of his considerable self-restraint not to do more. He caught himself wondering if Feiney was enjoying this. Knowing that scumbag, he was probably furious.

Though the temptation was strong, he wanted more when—if—he and Lea ever made love. He wanted it to be for real, not some sham thing they did out of frustration.

Oddly enough, at this point, judging from her wavering, Lea didn't care.

Therefore, it would be up to him to save her from both herself and from him. As long as she understood it was all part of the game, they'd be okay.

She shook her head. "Just don't, Marc. Okay?"

"Just don't what?" He forced the words out through clenched teeth, only partially acting. "Touch you? Make love to you?"

"I..."

"If you'd let me, I could chase every thought of that

slimy little bastard out of your head." He deliberately leered at her.

As he'd known they would, his words got an instant reaction.

"How? By having sex? Not freaking likely." Scorn dripped from her voice. He found himself feeling faint admiration, while summoning up outrage. Typical male, he told himself, act like a typical male, not like one who saw the truth in every icy word.

"Chicken," he taunted, using his eyes to try and tell her not to take anything he said seriously.

"Maybe I am." She shrugged. "But then again, so are you. I'm going to take a shower. Watch my phone." She gave him a polite little smile as she said it, but her smile didn't entirely reach her eyes.

"Feiney hasn't called in a while," he said, conscious of the ever-present camera, hoping to provoke the serial killer into doing exactly that.

"True." Though she continued smiling, worry darkened her eyes. "He won't know I'm in the shower," she lied. "But you'd better answer, just in case he does. It might be interesting to let you talk to him this time."

*Interesting* didn't even begin to describe it.

Barely two minutes after the bathroom door closed and the shower started up, Lea's cell phone rang.

Bingo. Which meant Feiney had not only been watching, but the bastard actually wanted to talk to Marc.

He picked it up, glancing at the caller ID. Unknown. Of course. "Hello."

Silence.

"I didn't take you for a coward," Marc said, hoping to goad him into speaking. "Getting tired?"

Feiney laughed, the guttural sound sending a chill up Marc's spine. His was the mad laughter one often heard around Halloween, in a cheesy haunted house, straight from a B-grade horror flick. In other words, the laughter of a madman.

But they'd already known that, right?

He steeled himself to hear what the man had to say.

"You screwed up."

Marc kept his tone conversational. "How so, Feiney?"

"There are so many ways I couldn't even begin to list them all."

"Starting with not being able to capture you yet, right?" Marc decided to play along. Then, just as insurance, he continued. "But we found your little cameras. Score one for my team."

He waited to see if Feiney would acknowledge the one they'd let stay.

"You only found the cameras because I told the woman I was watching her."

Uh-oh. *The woman*. Not Lea. Which meant Feiney was objectifying her. Most serial killers did this when they killed.

Marc decided to use her name. "You mean Lea?"

"Yeah, that bitch." Feiney spat the words. "She's mine."

Saying nothing, Marc waited.

"You're screwing her, aren't you?"

Aware Feiney was most likely also watching him on camera, Marc dragged his hand through his hair. "None of your business."

"It is my business," Feiney roared. "She is my business."

"The woman?" Marc said it this way as a test. He hoped Feiney would say Lea's name.

Instead, Feiney shouted one word into the phone. *"Mine."*

For a second, Marc held his breath, thinking Feiney was about to hang up on him. But then he heard another sound, a familiar voice that froze his blood.

"Lea? Dear God, don't let him hurt you, Lea. Don't worry about me, I'll be—"

Lea's mother. Marc reeled back, nearly fumbling the phone.

"You hear that?" Feiney sounded gleeful. "The bitch wouldn't trade with me before, but I bet she will now. Her for her mother. She has one hour to decide, or the old bat dies."

Then came the audible click of Feiney disconnecting the call.

Still clutching the phone, Marc heard the sound of the shower cutting off. In a few minutes, Lea was going to come through that door and he would have to tell her what had to be one of her worst nightmares. He'd have to tell her that her mother had been captured by the monster.

# Chapter 12

Lea emerged from the bathroom on a cloud of peach-scented steam. With her face scrubbed free of makeup and her hair in a towel turban, she looked all of twenty—beautiful and innocent and calm.

The instant she saw his face, her relaxed expression vanished.

"He called?"

Marc nodded, holding up a finger. Then, before he said another word, he went into the kitchen and grabbed the terra-cotta vase on top of the refrigerator. "I hope you're not too attached to this," he said. Not waiting for her response, he strode to the doorway, leaned over the landing and heaved the container toward the Dumpster. When it hit the pavement below, it shattered.

Returning to the apartment, he jerked his chin toward the door. "The camera's gone now."

She stood in the exact same spot, watching him. "I take it our masquerade got a reaction?"

Uncomfortable, he scratched the back of his head. "Yeah. Lea, he's got your mother."

"No, he doesn't," she responded instantly. "He's messing with you. I'll call her right now and you'll see. He's lying."

"Sugar, he put her on the phone."

Recoiling, she gasped. "No."

"I'm sorry." Intending to offer comfort, he reached for her. She evaded him easily, the wary look in her eyes frightening him more than the rage had.

"Why? What's he want with my mother?" Though she asked, Marc knew she already had the answer. When she let loose with a long string of curses strong enough to make a sailor blush, he knew she was just venting.

"I'll kill the lunatic." Raising her head, she met his gaze. The wariness, the frenzy had all morphed into a flat deadness. "He'd better not touch one hair on my mother's head, you understand?"

"I do, but Lea, you need to calm down. He's given us one hour. We've got to come up with a plan."

"One hour?" She snapped her head up. "One hour for what?"

He didn't want to tell her, but he had no choice. "To decide if you're willing to trade. Yourself for your mother."

As he'd known she would, she nodded immediately. "I don't need an hour. All he needs to tell me is when and where."

"Hold on." He thought furiously, trying to find the right words to make her think logically. "If we're not careful—"

"Screw careful."

He grabbed her, giving her a quick shake. "Listen to me. Please. If we make a wrong move he'll capture you and then make you watch him kill your mother. She'll die anyway. I know you don't want that."

He watched the light of battle leave her eyes. "You're right," she said slowly. "Then you've got to help me come up with a plan."

As she spoke, her cell phone started ringing.

"Feiney," she said, meeting Marc's gaze. "It hasn't even been half an hour. Why's he calling back?"

"Who knows? To torment you? Answer it," he urged, hating the resurgence of tension the call had brought to her face. The sooner they caught this bastard, the better. "But be careful. Stay in control."

Nodding, Lea answered, barely getting out a quick hello before falling silent. Feiney seemed to be doing all the talking. She simply listened, her jaw tensing more and more.

When she finally closed the phone, she looked at Marc and slowly shook her head. "He didn't want to talk about the trade, or my mother. Mostly, he wanted to vent. He was astounded you found that last camera. And he's furious." Her flat tone spoke of her own vehemence. "He didn't like you touching me or any of that. He says I belong to him. That I'm his fiancée and I'm cheating on him." She shuddered. "I can't tell you how much that creeps me out."

Marc nodded as though calm, though his insides were anything but. "Did he let you talk to your mom?"

He could see her visibly collecting herself. Finally, she swallowed. "No. He mentioned her in passing. Then, after he finished cursing at me, he said he's got a new directive for us."

"A directive?"

"Orders, whatever." She laughed, a humorless sound.

"He'll discuss the trade later. But first, he wants us to jump through hoops."

"He's—"

"Playing with us," she snarled. "I know that. We've got to get his location. I'm beginning to believe you're right. He has no intention of releasing my mother."

Part of him wanted to accept her words at face value. The other part thought her capitulation sounded a little too pat.

What was she up to?

He told himself it was his imagination. Had to be. Lea Cordasic was no fool.

"I hate that sick bastard," she muttered. "The thought of him touching my mother…"

He wanted to reach out to her, to offer what little comfort he could. Instead, he kept his hands at his sides and nodded. "We'll get her out safe."

"Damn straight we will." She gave him a dark look. "Feiney read me a poem he claims to have written." Though she struggled to keep her voice expressionless, a trace of her revulsion bled through.

"I'm his soul mate, we're meant for each other, blah, blah, blah. I honestly think he believes we're meant to be together. As if I'd ever really marry him." She cringed. "Blech."

Then, while he watched, she straightened her shoulders. "Let's get to work, Kenyon," she said briskly. The disgust so clear in her face a moment ago slowly transformed to what he thought of as her professional FBI agent, buttoned-up expression.

The Tarrant County sheriff part of him approved. The rest of him wanted simply to pull her into his arms and hold her while she cried.

"I hate that he's doing this. No." She held up her hand.

"Why me, Marc? Of all the women he kidnapped and killed, why did he let me live?"

He suspected she might ask that question a lot, especially since she'd been freed. Survivors often did, wondering what was so special about them that they'd lived while others had died. Survivor's guilt.

"He's emotionally involved, Lea. He believes you belong to him. He views our supposed relationship as wrong, as if I'm trespassing on his personal property."

Slowly, she nodded again. When she met his gaze, her own was cool and remote. "This is the kind of reaction you expected, right?"

"Hell, I didn't really think he'd go after your mother."

Briefly closing her eyes, she looked down. "I tried to warn her. I told her to get out of town, but she wouldn't listen." She released a quaking breath. "Now I'm going to have to call my brothers and tell them Feiney's got her. They're going to *kill* me."

Then she raised her head, determination showing in her eyes. "They'll both rush here, though. Come hell or high water. Dominic and Sebastian are good at what they do. Dom used to be a hostage negotiator and Seb was special ops." A dark shadow crossed her face. "They'll rush in, no holds barred, trying to rescue her. They'll get her killed."

From what he'd heard of her brothers, he doubted they'd do anything so foolish and said so. "You've got to tell them."

"No, I don't. There's not enough time. I'll take care of it myself." Again, he approved of her calmness, though he couldn't help but worry about how remote she appeared.

"Ourselves," he corrected. "We'll take care of it ourselves."

Again, she gave him that distant stare. Terror, rage

and something else lurked in the back of her expressive hazel eyes. He understood the fear and anger, but didn't understand the other feeling. Again, he got the sense that she was holding out on him. That she wanted him to think that they were still a team, moving forward in the right direction, while she carried out plans of her own.

"What are you not telling me?" he asked, his look daring her to lie to his face. His blood went cold at the stark look in her eyes. "Don't even think about hiding something from me. Explain."

She swallowed and then, raising her chin, began to recite the words. "To punish us, he says he's going to start cutting on her. One finger for each hour we make him wait for what he wants." The horror in her voice matched his.

"Damn it," Marc cursed. "He didn't say anything like that to me. All he mentioned was a trade."

"I'm guessing he wants to expedite things." She held up her hand.

Here it came. "What do you mean?"

"When he said an hour to decide, he meant *before* he started cutting. But if I do what he wants before an hour has passed, he won't touch her."

He said the first thing that came to mind. "I don't like this. At all. He's still toying with us. He's setting a trap."

"Possibly." She didn't sound too concerned. "Either way, what choice do we have? We have to try to save her."

"Letting him kill you won't do your mother any good."

Lifting her chin, she met his gaze straight on. "We have no choice, and he knows it. If he's telling the truth and we don't do what he wants, she's dead."

And there she had him. As law enforcement officials, they really had no options. Unless they could utilize the team. Maybe he could figure out a way. Though Lea wouldn't like it, Marc knew he'd do whatever he could to catch Feiney and keep her safe. The time deadline was the biggest obstacle.

"Let's hear the particulars. How does he want to make the swap?"

"Before I get to that, there's more. He doesn't want to trade me for my mom within an hour—he's leading up to that."

It bothered him that she didn't answer his question. For their careers as peace officers, they both understood classic avoidance tactics. Still, because he was curious to hear what else Feiney wanted, Marc followed her lead.

"I'll bite. What else does he want?"

"More media coverage, for one. He's written a letter to the media and wants me to read it on the air. He's requesting all major networks carry it."

Which he'd get. Serial killers, especially ones with hostages, were big news. Feiney didn't even have to ask for this.

Which meant she was still holding back, keeping something else from him. Something big. "That's it? Media coverage is a given and he knows it. You're holding back on me. Give me the rest of it."

She took a deep breath, then motioned him over. When he was right in front of her, she whispered in his ear. "He wants you dead."

"What?"

"He wants me to kill you."

"Now we're getting somewhere." He cocked his head. "Why are you whispering? Feiney can't see or hear us. I destroyed the remaining camera."

"That's just it. That camera you destroyed wasn't the only one left behind."

"It has to be. Stan said that team was one of the best."

Turning a slow circle in the room, she waited until she faced him again to continue. "Marc, I have to believe him when he says he's got another camera. The team must have missed it. It happens." Still she sounded strangely unconcerned. "Bottom line—he's watching us now."

All at once, Feiney's plan fell into place.

A second later, Lea confirmed it. "He says he'll come get me and leave my mother in trade, but only once he's watched me kill you."

His blood ran cold. "What are you going to do?"

"I have no clue," she said, her eyes glassy. "But I can't let my mother die."

"We'll figure something out." Cupping her chin in his hands, he searched her face. "This is our chance to finally capture the SOB. We'll get your mother out safely."

"I wish I could believe that."

Her phone chirped—a text message. Without changing expression, she read directly from the screen. "Feiney says I have thirty minutes."

Which meant they had to think fast. "Come on." He clasped her hand. "Outside."

Where Feiney couldn't hear.

Closing the door behind them, he turned to her. "We can make this work. If we set it up right—"

"First off, I wouldn't be surprised if he didn't have the landing here bugged, too."

"Lea, he's not all powerful."

"Maybe not, but it sure feels that way."

"You know he's lying." Wearily, he dragged his hand across his eyes. "He just wants to humiliate you, to teach you—and me—a lesson. He knows you won't kill me. Therefore, he won't do the trade. Nor will he let himself be captured so easily."

"You're saying he's going to kill my mother no matter what I do."

While he couldn't let her give up hope, she no longer sounded rational. "It's a distinct possibility."

Devastated, she crossed her arms and looked away.

Furious at the impossible position Feiney had put them in, Marc began to pace. The small landing outside her apartment didn't have enough room and for the first time, he understood her love of running.

"He's toying with us," he reiterated, squinting at her. "Did you ever study profiling?"

This got a startled look. "No."

"Well, this is classic. He's offering up a pretend scenario he knows we can't take."

"So he can make himself feel vindicated when he kills my mother?" she asked.

"Maybe." This stopped him short. "Did he ever need validation before?"

"No." She thought for a moment. "At least, not that I know of. Of course, during the time he held me prisoner, he used me as his sounding board."

"Seeking your approval."

"Which I never gave." She sounded horrified. A moment later, she nodded. "I never thought about it, but I guess you could be right. In a way I suppose he was trying to impress me." She shivered. "As if."

"I'm sorry. I know how difficult this must be for you." Crossing to her, he took her arm. "But Lea, you're the key. Right now, you've become Feiney's motivating force. We've got to figure out a way to force him to play his hand."

"Poker analogies?" For a moment, she stared at him, saying nothing else. Finally, she looked away. When he moved forward, she let him lead her downstairs, keeping pace easily with his longer stride. Mulling over his words.

"Force him how?" she finally asked, glancing around her as though she expected Feiney had eyes everywhere, watching.

"He can't see you."

"Just say what you want to say," she spat. "The clock is ticking."

Relieved that she still had her fighting spirit, he squeezed her shoulder. "There's got to be a way we can turn his plan against him."

"Well, if you're going to come up with something, you'd better think of it quickly. We have less than thirty minutes!" Despite the briskness of her steps, she sounded tired.

"What I don't understand is how Feiney can actually believe…"

"He's a demented serial killer." She shook her head. "There is no understanding how someone like him thinks."

"All that matters is that we beat him at his own game."

At his words, she squared her shoulders and lifted her chin. "Thanks. I needed that."

Relief flooded him. He'd said exactly the right thing to bring her out of her dark cloud. Standing at the bottom of the steps leading to her apartment, a light breeze ruffling her hair, he'd never seen a more beautiful woman.

Dang, he was getting in deep. He needed to take a step back and be more careful or Feiney wouldn't be the only one hurt by the time this operation was over.

Shaking off his unexpected melancholy, he took a deep breath. "We need more time to come up with a plan."

"Time we don't have."

"Then you're going to have to do it. Kill me off."

"What?" She stopped in her tracks, her hazel eyes wide and shocked.

"Not for real. If we can stage my death, we might be able to fool him. If we can do that, we could draw him out. Then we'd stand a shot of capturing him."

One hand on the lamp pole, she glanced back up at the landing, almost as if she expected Feiney to appear. Finally, her gaze came back to Marc and she nodded. "Keep talking."

"I'm going off the top of my head. We go back inside and stage a fight. A horrible, nasty fight."

"Go on." Her dubious look would have been comical, if the situation hadn't been so urgent.

"We escalate things to the point where you kill me."

"What?" She took a step back. "Are you crazy? Do you really think he'll buy that?"

"Why not? He asked for you to kill me. Be creative. Think outside the box. Feiney won't expect that."

Arms crossed, she stared at him.

"You kill me," he repeated. "Pretend to, I mean. In the heat of passion. When I'm dead, you can cry and say you did it to save your mother, but now you're as bad as him. How you realize you still love him."

She recoiled in horror. "I'd never say anything like that. Not in a million years."

"You know that, I know that. But Feiney doesn't. He thinks you two are destined to be together. Convince him you really love him and nothing on earth will stand in the way of him coming to retrieve you."

"You honestly believe…"

"It's our only chance." He took a deep breath, feeling his certainty build. "We're dealing with a deranged psychopath.

This is the only way I can think of to satisfy him and keep him from cutting your mom every hour."

"It might work." She still sounded doubtful.

He challenged her. "What have we got to lose?"

"It's pretty far-fetched."

"True, but if you've got a better plan, tell me now."

"You know I don't." Resigned, she shook her head. "If we do this, we've got to make it believable."

Her phone chimed again. "Twenty minutes."

"Can you do this?" He studied her face, wondering if she'd actually be able to carry out their plan.

She nodded. "I can do it. Yes. What about you?"

"It's just one more undercover assignment. I've had to do worse."

"Me, too. But still. This is messed up."

"We're just giving him what he wants. On the surface. But you've got to be ready for him when he shows up. Follow me?"

"Yes." She gave him a grim smile. "Okay, okay. You win. Since time is running out, tell me, what did you have in mind as far as, uh, me killing you?"

At least she was on board. Although reluctantly. Actually, he couldn't blame her. Hell, it was his plan and even he wasn't sure it was a smart one.

Bottom line—did he trust her? He really must, because it sure as hell sounded like he was offering himself up as some sort of sacrificial lamb.

Again, what choice did they have?

"I thought you'd just shoot me with your service pistol. Of course the gun would be loaded with blanks. It'd help if we had a fake blood bag, just like in the movies. If we play it right, we could convince him."

"We don't have time to gather up props."

Glancing at his watch, he grimaced. "I know. You're right."

He thought for a moment. "Let's get back to the apartment. Stage the fight, stab me. If you position the knife right…"

"Fine." He could tell she didn't like the idea, but it was all they had. "What are we going to argue about?"

"The plan. We need to discuss this in front of Feiney. He says he'll trade your mom for you. We both know he's lying, but what if you act like you think you can convince him to really do that? And I argue against it."

"I'm still listening." Crossing her arms, she regarded him with narrowed eyes.

"We go for it."

"I'm not sure I like where this is going."

"We make him believe you'd actually kill me, in the heat of this argument. We can make it believable."

"I'm not shooting you." Out came the chin. "Or stabbing you."

"Club me over the head then, I don't care. As long as you make it believable."

"He'll never buy it. How about I don't kill you at all. What if we argue, I stun you and knock you out, then I can tie you up and tell Feiney we're on for the trade. You won't be able to stop me." She looked over at him. "That's better than killing you. Because then he'll have the pleasure of killing you himself."

He raised a brow. "There's only one problem with his scenario. He'll never believe you could overpower me. I've got a hundred pounds on you, easily."

Her phone pinged again. "Fifteen minutes. Damn."

He frowned. "Explain to me how you plan to overpower me and we'll go inside and do it."

"I can take you if you're distracted. Like if we're

kissing." Though she turned bright red, she doggedly continued. "Plus, I have training in martial arts."

Training might be an understatement. He'd heard she was a black belt.

"Put that way…" With a dip of his head, he conceded the point. "We'll go with your plan."

"All right then. Plan of action decided. Let's go."

Hanging back, he gave her a sideways look. "How good an actress are you?"

Taking a deep breath, she hesitated. "I… Pretty good." She lifted her chin, appearing to gain confidence. "I just have to hang on to how much I despise Feiney. I can do this. I know I can."

"Do you know what?" Though he wanted to kiss her, he settled for a light touch on her shoulder. "I believe you can. Whatever you do to me, I'll pretend it's worse. Let's go."

"Okay." Her answering smile, though wobbly and uncertain, felt like a punch to the chest. "One, two, three, let's do it."

## Chapter 13

Pretending to kill Marc or at least overpower him was not only the strangest idea Lea had ever heard, but quite possibly the only one that might work. Feiney would never expect this much creativity from a pair of buttoned-down law-enforcement officers. Not in a million years. Hell, Lea had trouble believing it herself.

In fact, she suspected this was the only reason she'd agreed to such a wild and crazy plan. The sheer outrageousness of it practically guaranteed it would work. That and the fact that she had no alternative.

Hopefully, Feiney would believe it.

She prayed he stuck to his ridiculously short time frame and that he hadn't yet harmed her mother. She wouldn't be responsible for her own actions if he had.

Concentrate, she told herself. Focus on what you can control. Pretending to knock Marc out was a million-to-one shot, and if Feiney didn't buy it, they'd be right back where they'd started. Nowhere.

Now to get in character. Marc would help her with that. She realized with some surprise that she completely trusted him. Still wanted him, though that desire had of course been relegated to a secret, private part of herself. Maybe, once they got past this and Feiney had been returned to prison, she'd take it out and examine it. Perhaps even allow something to come of it. Who knew?

For now, her focus had to be on this. Acts one, two and three, all rolled into one.

Since they had less than ten minutes remaining before Feiney called in his marker and cut off her mother's finger, right now she had to concentrate and do this. She could do this. For this miniature play, Marc would become the enemy and all she had was herself. Her anger, her rage, her fury. Her absolute, unshakable hatred of Feiney.

In the apartment, she paced, constantly checking her watch.

"Calm down," Marc told her, appearing supremely unruffled, hands in pockets, slouching on the couch.

"He hasn't called. Why hasn't he called?" Since she didn't know where the camera was this time, she couldn't play to that. "He's late."

"So?" Marc deadpanned. "Five minutes is nothing. What's time to a serial killer?"

Gritting her teeth, she rounded on him. "How dare you! Time might not be anything to Feiney, but it's everything to me. This is my mother he's got now."

"Calm down. It'll be all right."

"It occurs to me that I should try to call her." She pulled out her cell phone, opened it and punched in her mother's number. "Why should I take your word that you talked to her when Feiney called?"

The call went straight to voice mail.

Impassive, Marc watched her close her phone. "Satisfied now?" he asked softly. "If you're done questioning my integrity, maybe we can focus on coming up with a solution."

Though she knew the entire conversation was an act, it felt like it was getting more personal, more real, than she'd thought it would be.

She hadn't expected the barbs to sting quite so badly.

"Maybe we can," she retorted. "Assuming Feiney sticks to the time schedule he gave you. Or did you possibly misunderstand that, too?"

"Too?" Crossing his arms, he cocked his head. "What are you implying?"

"I don't know." She began pacing again, wishing she had more room to stretch her legs, more room to run. "I hate dealing with someone whose word can't be trusted."

"He'll do what he said."

"How do you know this?" she asked, unable to mask her wrath and her pain. "What magic crystal ball tells you that Feiney won't send my mother's hand back to me in pieces, right before he dumps her body, all without giving me a chance to take her place?"

He pushed himself to his feet. "Lea, you need to settle down. This is not the way to deal with this crisis. You need to—"

Cutting him off with a look that would have melted steel, she shook her head. "You have your methods and I have mine. Don't tell me how to act. You don't have nearly as much at stake as I do."

"Maybe not, but I do care," he said, his voice unbearably gentle. This made her falter. She sensed he was actually telling the truth, not acting. Bad move and one that frightened her so badly she grew even more incensed.

"Well, don't."

"Don't what?"

"Care." She glared at him. "I don't want you to care. He has *my mother.* She wouldn't leave and she thought I'd protect her." More truth. This improved acting could be more dangerous than either of them had realized, in more ways than one. Still, she'd chosen a path and now had no choice but to take it.

"It's all my fault," she continued. "I screwed up again."

"No." The hard lines in his handsome face didn't soften. "You have no reason to feel guilty. If—"

"No reason?" Familiar rage filled her. She allowed it, welcoming it and letting it deepen. "Don't tell me I have no reason. Who are you to think—"

"I'm the one who's going to get Feiney," he snarled. "So don't worry your pretty little head about it."

To her amazement, she nearly lost it then and there, even knowing this was all staged. But losing her cool would only lead to more intimately personal details becoming revealed—to both Marc as well as Feiney—and she wanted to avoid that if at all possible.

Instead, she mentally took a step back. "I think we both need to calm down," she said, using a measured, even tone.

Marc did the absolute worst possible thing—or the best, depending on the point of view. Staring at her, he laughed.

A hearty, masculine laugh, the kind a man makes when he thinks a woman is a complete, incompetent idiot. The kind practically guaranteed to set her blood boiling.

Still, despite the flash of fury, she still was clearheaded enough to realize she needed to try to plan ahead to the next step. Pretend to kill him? Or pretend to overpower him and knock him out, then tie him up?

Maybe he was waiting for her.

"He should have called by now." She checked her watch yet again. "It's been a full ten minutes since he was supposed to call me back for an answer."

Marc grabbed her shoulder. "An answer to what?"

"Let go," she yelped. Then, hoping she didn't hurt him, she took him down at the knees. He went over like a ton of bricks, his head slamming against the side of her end table.

"Marc?"

He didn't move. Heart pounding so hard she thought it might burst from her chest, she reminded herself that he'd said he'd feign unconsciousness.

Glad he hadn't worn his sheriff's uniform with the regulation handcuffs, she went to her bedroom in search of something to use to tie him up. Something she could rig loosely so he could free himself when the time came.

She'd just settled on two of her old belts when her cell phone rang and she nearly jumped out of her skin.

Feiney.

"Hello?"

"What are you doing?" he hissed. "He's down, he's out. Finish him off."

"I'm looking for something to use to tie him up, in case he comes to." Heaven help her, she nearly choked on the words she had to say next. "I thought you'd like to do that. Kill him, I mean. It's sort of what you specialize in, isn't it?" She gave a self-conscious, utterly false-sounding laugh.

The line went quiet while he considered.

Damn. She didn't want him to take time to think.

"Put my mother on the line," she demanded. "I want to talk to her and make sure she's still alive."

"You don't give orders to me."

"Cut the crap, Feiney. Put her on right now or I'm assuming she's dead and the deal's off."

"Deal?" His voice rolled over her, oily and serpentine, and she suppressed a shudder. "I wasn't aware you'd agreed to my terms."

"You never called back for me to tell you." Keeping her voice even, she lobbed the ball into his court. "I'm agreeing to the trade. Even better, it's two for one."

"I told you to kill him."

"I can't." Truth whenever possible always worked better than lies, especially to sweeten a deal. "If you want him dead, you'll have to do it yourself. Two birds for one stone. Me, and you get to kill Marc."

For the space of a few heartbeats, he said nothing. She refused to be the one to break the silence.

"I don't believe you." He sounded suspicious, as well he should be. Feiney might be many things, but he wasn't stupid.

Neither was she.

"Then that makes two of us. I don't believe you, either. Let me talk to my mother or the deal's off."

Holding her breath, she waited for him to decide.

Then Lillian Cordasic's voice came over the line. "Don't worry about me, honey. I'm fine."

"Mom," Lea breathed, "Has he touched you?"

"No."

But there had been the barest hesitation, enough to make Lea wonder. "I'm gonna get you out of there, do you hear me?"

"I'm fine. Lea, I—" Her mother screamed, a shrill sound

so full of pain and so unlike her that Lea had to clutch at her stomach with one hand to keep from doubling over.

"Mom? Mom?"

"Run!" Lillian shouted. The next thing Lea heard was the click of the call being disconnected.

Immediately, she hit redial, only to get a recorded message saying the call could not be completed as dialed.

"Damn it." Wanting to kick something, punch something, she restrained herself from throwing the phone into the wall. Lot of good that would do.

The two belts she'd taken out of her closet caught her eye. Should she go tie Marc up or not bother? Feiney's lack of direction or instruction was seriously pissing her off. Each passing second that her mother remained in his hands...

The thought was too unbearable to contemplate.

Out of her control. Not acceptable.

Snatching up the belts, she went back into the other room to see if Marc was still unconscious or, rather, feigning unconsciousness.

He hadn't moved. This was both good and bad.

Just in case, she pulled his arms behind him and wrapped the first of the belts around him, right above the elbow. The second she twined around his wrists, careful to give him enough wiggle room. Since she had no idea where the camera was situated, she didn't dare try to communicate with him, just in case Feiney was watching and listening.

Standing, she eyed her handiwork, trying for an objective eye. She needed one more belt, to make it look like Marc was securely tied, while in actuality he wouldn't be. She headed back to her bedroom. Halfway there, she heard a sound and froze.

Listening, she waited for it to come again.

Cursing her shot nerves, she continued into her bedroom, moving toward the closet.

"Hello, darling Lea."

Feiney stood in the entrance to the closet, holding a pistol that she recognized as a Glock nine millimeter, pointed directly at her.

The sight stopped her in her tracks.

Damn. Pulse battering her chest, she stared. Once again, he'd managed to surprise her. But she couldn't let this give him the upper hand.

"How'd you get in here?" she asked, sounding cool, calm, and collected.

"From the apartment next door. The closets join. I came in through the ceiling tiles."

He shouldn't have been able to still horrify her, but she couldn't help glancing at the wall separating her apartment from the other. "What happened to Mrs. Pachla?" The friendly elderly woman had lived there before Lea had even moved in.

Feiney's slow grin gave answer enough.

"Oh no." She blinked. "You killed Mrs. Pachla?"

"Why do you sound surprised?" His smile widened, though his brown eyes were coldly serious. "Killing is what I do."

Put that way, he was absolutely correct. A psychopathic serial killer killed. Only a complete idiot would expect him to act differently.

But if she wanted to make it through this, to save her mother and herself—not to mention Marc—and capture Feiney, she sure as hell had to pretend to be severely lacking in mental capacity.

Meeting his gaze dead-on and not flinching took an extraordinary amount of self-control. Oddly enough, the fact that she could even do this gave her a burst of confidence.

"Where's my mother?" she demanded.

"Safe."

She crossed her arms, willing her inner trembling to subside. "I want to see her."

"Your wants no longer count for anything." He waved the pistol. "You have nothing left to bargain with. Go back into the living room."

Clenching her teeth, she turned and marched ahead of him.

Marc still lay on the floor, unmoving and unresponsive.

"Are you sure you didn't kill him?" Feiney alternated his gaze between Lea and Marc. "While that would save me a lot of trouble, it would also remove quite a bit of the fun factor."

Fun factor. She had a brief and terrible mental picture of her hands around his throat, choking him. Fun factor indeed.

She needed to accomplish two things. One, to get Feiney to bring her mother here and two, to get him to leave alone with her.

Only then would she have a chance to take him down without risking either Marc or her mom's life.

And only that way could she ensure that she would be the only casualty if she failed.

Failure was not an option.

Turning to face Feiney, she eyed him and the Glock. "Let me see my mother or the deal's off."

"I told you, you have nothing to bargain with," he sneered.

"Oh, but I do. Either bring my mother, or I'm going to

rush you and your weapon. You'll have to shoot to kill, Feiney. Or I'm taking you down."

He studied her with narrowed eyes, possibly trying to gauge her seriousness.

To make sure he understood, she took a step toward him.

"I mean it."

To her surprise and disbelief, he took a step back. Though he didn't lower the gun. "If I let you see your mother, you'll swear in her blood to become my wife?"

His choice of words alarmed her. "In her blood? What have you done to my mother?"

"Lower your voice," he snapped, waving the gun at her. "She has a few small cuts and bruises. Nothing serious."

"For your sake you'd better be telling the truth."

His brown eyes went flat and cold. "Or what? I could shoot you now, shoot him, too." He indicated Marc with a jerk of his head. "Then I could go next door and have my fun with your dear old mommy before I kill her as well. Then, I'd be out of here. And your cops would never catch me."

Steeling herself, she moved forward, only stopping when the muzzle of his Glock was pressed flat against her chest. "Do it, then. Go ahead, pull the trigger. Because you know what, Feiney? I don't really give a damn if I live or I die."

She breathed in, breathed out, her gaze locked on his. The steady rhythm of her heart surprised her, as did the fact that she was no longer afraid. Her ever-present anger, always her nemesis, sustained her, enabling her to turn her body, shift her weight and twist her leg around his to bring the scumbag down.

As he fell, she rolled right, bringing her left arm up

to knock the gun out of his grip. He squeezed off a shot, which went wild, taking out her dresser mirror.

The gun hit the dresser drawer, spinning just out of Feiney's reach. Elbowing him hard enough to knock the wind from him, Lea went for the weapon.

As her fingers closed around it, she realized for the first time that she just might actually win. She had the power to ensure that Feiney would never again capture another unsuspecting woman and rape and torture her. In fact, if she wanted to, she could make certain Feiney would no longer disgrace the earth with the stench of his presence.

White-hot rage filled her as, Glock in hand, she rolled and threw her full weight on top of him. Slamming his head into the carpet, gun to his head, she realized she could so easily kill him and claim self-defense.

Bye-bye, Feiney.

The temptation—sharp and swift—made her realize a part of her had the inherent potential to do to him what he'd done to her and the others. To become, in effect, as lawless and evil as he.

Her sense of moral certitude combined with her martial arts training and law-enforcement education brought her back from the brink just in time. Lucky for him.

"No," she gasped, keeping the pistol trained on him as she climbed to her feet. "I won't become the same as you."

"Reinforcements are on the way." Marc's voice came from behind her. "They've got the building surrounded."

"Good." Her toneless voice sounded professional. She refused to tear her gaze from Feiney. "Don't move."

Marc came up to stand next to her with his own weapon drawn. "I've got your back."

"Of course you do," she said. And meant it.

"I've asked them to send men next door to rescue your mom."

Dipping her chin in a quick nod, she muttered a quiet prayer that Lillian was still alive.

When he'd heard the gun go off, Marc had feared the worst. Taking the few seconds to get free of the belts Lea had used to tie him felt like an eternity. He'd reached the bedroom door just as she'd taken Feiney down.

Unaware of him standing behind her, she'd flickered dangerously close to the edge of losing self-control. He'd identified with that. If she'd killed Feiney with her bare hands, he wondered if he'd have tried to stop her. Hell, part of him had wanted to be the one with the hands around the sick bastard's throat.

What she'd said about not wanting to turn into Feiney had made him realize she wouldn't, any more than he would.

Feiney was going back to prison.

And Marc could only wonder where he and Lea were heading.

In the apartment next door, they'd found Lea's mother, tied and gagged, but alive. On the floor next to her lay the body of Mrs. Pachla, a woman in her mid-eighties who apparently had no superficial trauma. He'd bet once the M.E. got through with her, they'd learn she'd expired of a heart attack or some other such thing. No doubt brought on by Feiney, but unable to be proven.

"Mom." Openly weeping, Lea gently pried off the duct tape gag, then fumbled with the ropes binding her mother. "Oh, Mom, are you okay?"

Shakily, Lillian Cordasic climbed to her feet. Hugging Lea back, she peered at Marc before wiping at her own eyes, which were also leaking tears.

"Where is he? Where is that sorry excuse for a man?" Hands bunched into fists, balancing on the balls of her small feet, the older woman appeared ready for a fistfight.

Marc grinned. "You mean Feiney?"

"Exactly."

"Your daughter took him down. Right now he's in custody."

"Fantastic." Turning to Lea, Lillian raised one hand to ask for a shaky but jubilant high five. "Way to go."

"Yeah." Sniffling, Lea grabbed her mom for another hug. "I'm so glad he didn't hurt you."

"He tried, honey. But I gave him what for. When I told him how angry you were going to be, he left me alone."

Brushing away tears, Lea met Marc's gaze. "Tough old lady," he mouthed.

Apparently not quietly enough. "Who are you calling old?" Lillian demanded.

And with that, they all laughed.

They were still laughing when the full contingent of uniformed officers and FBI agents descended to take them in for questioning.

Hours later, debriefed and thoroughly examined by medical personnel, they were finally fed sandwiches from a nearby sub shop and then released. Both Marc and Lea declined an offer to participate in a press conference that had been scheduled for 4:30 p.m., just in time to make the five o'clock news.

They were delivered back to Lea's apartment in an unmarked patrol car.

"I want to go home," Lillian demanded, as soon as they got out of the car.

"Mom, I don't think you should be alone tonight." Wrapping an arm around her mother's slender shoulder, Lea hugged her.

"Who said anything about being alone?"

Surprised, Lea drew back to peer at her mother's face. "What do you mean?"

"Oh, didn't I tell you? I guess I forgot in all that's been going on. Your brothers and their wives are on their way in. They'll all be here tonight for a late supper. You need to come around seven."

"Oh, Mom. Surely you're not cooking?"

"Heavens, no. I'm sending out for pizza. I expect you and Marc to be there."

Face burning, Lea glanced at Marc. "Mom, Marc might have other plans. He—"

"Of course I'll be there, Mrs. Cordasic," Marc interrupted smoothly. "I wouldn't miss it for the world."

Lea shot him a look that meant they needed to talk, hoping he'd interpret it correctly.

Apparently he did.

"Let's run your mom home, Lea. Then we can come back home, er...here and get ready for tonight."

Woodenly, she nodded. Though she really needed time to herself, time to recover and reassess that she'd done the right thing, she needed to see her two older brothers more. Family was family, and more than any other family, the Cordasic's history in law enforcement meant they truly understood what she'd just gone through.

And, she reflected ruefully, if she even thought about skipping out on tonight, one or both of her brothers would come and get her.

But if she brought Marc, they'd all assume...

Listening with half an ear as her mother chattered happily, Lea reflected that her mother already did assume.

Poor Marc. He had no idea what he was in for.

She'd have to warn him and figure out a way to give him a graceful out, no hard feelings.

Otherwise, the family would assume their relationship—a pretend thing fashioned with the intent of capturing a serial killer—was not only real, but serious.

She wanted to groan, but truthfully, after what she'd just been through, this was gravy. Almost a relief, to focus on normal things. A huge weight had been lifted off her back.

With a sense of dawning clarity, she knew she'd go back to therapy a few more times and be quickly cleared to return to work. Working with Marc and the ultimate confrontation with Feiney had proved to her that she still had what it took to work for her beloved FBI.

In his own twisted way, Feiney's escape from prison had healed her.

Settling back in her seat while Marc drove, she thought she just might go to Vegas for a vacation before she returned to work. She'd always loved the city and since Dom, Rachel and her son Cole lived there, that gave the place an extra bonus.

Marc's cell phone rang and he took the call, pulling up in front of Lillian's home. At Lea's questioning look, he waved them away, still on the phone while Lea escorted her mother into the house.

When she returned ten minutes later, narrowly escaping being placed on bathroom cleaning detail, he concluded his call and looked at her. "Everything all right?"

"Yep, although I'm beat," she told him. "Would you mind taking me back to my place so I can get cleaned up and rest before this shindig tonight?"

*Her place.* Now, she realized, they would each resume living their separate lives, in their different apartments.

She felt an odd twinge of loss in her chest, and put it away to examine later.

Marc nodded, his expression shuttered. "Of course." He put the car in Drive and pulled out into the street.

It seemed weird to have to act so formal, but she saw no way around it. "You're welcome to come up. After all, you still have to…"

"Get my stuff," he said. "I know."

Relieved, she let her eyes drift closed. Sleepily, she made a mental note to mention to him the family's certain expectations if he accompanied her later tonight.

"Lea, wake up. We're here." Marc's voice, his warm breath in her ear.

She murmured something, stretched and yawned. Her eyelids felt heavy, but she forced them open and peered blearily up into his baby-blue eyes.

"We're at your apartment," he repeated, pulling back slightly, his gaze darkening as he watched her. "Can you make it up the stairs?"

Nearly giddy with exhaustion, she chuckled. "I beat a serial killer earlier. What's a few flights of stairs?"

He shook his head and got out of the car, pocketing the keys before crossing to her side to open her door. Then, as she was struggling to climb out of the seat, he pulled her up against him. Feeling his arousal, she blinked, suddenly wide-awake and dry-mouthed.

"Uh, Marc? There's something we need to talk about," she began.

Covering her mouth in a quick, hard kiss, he shook his head. "Let's get inside. There's a lot more I want to do than just talk."

# Chapter 14

Her entire body tingling from the promise implicit in Marc's husky voice, Lea followed him up the stairs on shaky legs. Fumbling with her keys, she unlocked her door, stepping inside and letting him in past her.

Breathing ridiculously fast, she locked the door, fussing with the dead bolt and triple-checking the lock before finally turning to face him. Her heart turned over at the tender hunger she saw in his eyes.

"Am I wrong?" he asked, his blue gaze serious. "If I am, say so now, and I'll leave."

Stomach tingling, she didn't even have to ask what he meant. They both knew about the heat that flared between him. Whether or not she wanted to test its flame, he was leaving it up to her.

The very space between them felt electrified. Her chest ached, her insides jangled and she couldn't seem to find the right words.

But then she knew no words were actually necessary.

She could take a man out with just her hands, shoot a target dead-center with one shot, but she couldn't make herself give in to impulse, or give in to desire, and cross the distance between them. She couldn't let herself do what she wanted and put her mouth on his and her arms around his neck.

Instead, she stood wanting, needing, burning.

And Marc turned to go.

"Wait." She held out her hand. "After what happened with Feiney…" Swallowing hard, she tried to find the right way to explain.

"I understand. You're not ready."

"Marc. Freeze. Hold up."

Slowly, he turned to face her.

"After Feiney, I wondered if I'd ever be able to let a man touch me again. Ever. But with you, it's different. I feel… normal. Sexy. Wanted. Please don't go."

He cocked his head, watching her, waiting.

Closing her eyes, she let the last of her fear and pride fall away. "I want you, Marc Kenyon. Make love to me."

Crossing the room, he moved so fast she barely had time to react. Cupping her face in his large hands, holding her hard so she couldn't move, yet so gently she could feel the calluses on his fingers, he covered her mouth with his.

"Ahhh." Now she found words, whispering them against his lips. "I'm so glad you did that."

He smothered the last words with his mouth, demanding, kissing her with a pent-up hunger that told her he wanted her as fiercely as she wanted him.

Like a flower blooming under a warm spring sun, she opened herself to him, allowing his solid strength to wash over her and finally cleanse the last lingering fragment of the insidious rage left from Feiney.

She couldn't mark the exact moment when the kiss changed, but change it did. The warmth went from a slow burn to an outright inferno. Somehow, she found herself with her arms wrapped around his neck, pulling him closer. His arousal pressed against her and this time, rather than moving away, she moved into him, letting him feel her own desire in the movement of her body.

As the heat between them built to a feverish intensity, she reached for the button on his jeans.

"Wait." He grabbed her hand, holding her away.

Then, while she muttered a desire-fogged sound of protest, he led her back to the guest bedroom.

"Why here?" she protested.

"Because the camera is still up, and we don't know where it is." Releasing her hand, he used his own to stroke her, sending shivers of pleasure through her.

"Oh." She said the only thing she could think of.

"I don't want to put on a show for the entire FBI."

"Good thinking." Location already forgotten, she explored his muscular chest and shoulders, running her hand down the length of his arm.

"Have I told you how beautiful you are?" she murmured.

"That goes both ways." Capturing her lips again, he gave her a long, deep, drugging kiss.

When he began to unbutton her blouse, she helped him. Then, fingers trembling, she fumbled with his shirt, letting out a soft cry as he unbuckled her bra, letting her breasts spill into his hands.

*Finally.*

"I want to see you naked," she told him, fiercely intent, grabbing at the waistband of his jeans.

He chuckled, pulling her in again for a kiss. "Slowly. We've waited for this a long time."

Impatient, she shook her head, sending her hair flying in a curtain around them, writhing against him, unable to keep from smiling as he gave an involuntary jerk against her.

"Slowly, huh? I don't want slowly." She nipped at his neck, then his earlobe, enjoying the way he shuddered as she whispered in his ear. "I want fast and hot and heavy."

As she spoke, she yanked his jeans open, freeing him in all his aroused magnificence. "Wow."

Hand trembling, she wrapped her hand around him, caressing him once, twice, until he grabbed her fingers and stopped her.

Gently, almost reverently, he removed her panties and then, when they both were naked, ushered her into his arms and held her.

"Give me a minute," he groaned, holding her still though his body involuntarily twitched against her.

She did, reveling in the feel of his hard masculinity, the perfect fit of their bodies. As they held each other close, she realized with a sort of stunned amazement that tears of happiness pricked the back of her eyes.

When he pulled her with him back onto the bed, she went gladly, boldly letting herself explore him intimately. When he bent his head to her nipple, she gasped, then opened her legs as he lowered himself over her and she accepted him joyously inside her.

He filled her, and as he began to move inside her, increasing the tempo steadily, she felt herself unraveling piece by piece. When she shattered into a million exploding stars, he was right there with her.

After, he held her and she held him back, their damp bodies cooling gradually, neither willing to move away.

"Marc," she began, only to be silenced by a slow, lingering kiss.

"Not now," he told her. "We'll talk later. For now, let's just enjoy this moment."

So she did.

When she opened her eyes again, still nestled in the curve of his body, she lifted herself up on her elbow to peer at the clock.

"Oh, no." She nudged him awake. "Marc, we must have fallen asleep. It's nearly six. We've got a little more than an hour until we have to be at my mother's house."

He groaned and rolled over, burrowing his face into the pillow. "You take the first shower. Wake me when it's my turn."

"Oh." She let her disappointment show in her voice. "I was hoping we could shower together. You know, wash each other off. I thought it'd go faster that way."

Now she had his attention. He sat up fast, grabbing for her. She laughed as she danced out of his way.

"Race you there," she said, already halfway to the bathroom.

"I hope you know we're going to be late," he warned her, catching her before she even turned on the water.

Later, Lea dried her hair while Marc phoned her mother to let her know they were running a bit late. By some miracle they made it out the front door at 7:10.

"By the time we get there, we'll only be half an hour late." Lea smiled, letting her gaze roam over Marc as he drove. He seemed distracted, preoccupied, and she couldn't help but wonder if the daunting prospect of meeting her family bothered him.

"I haven't seen my brothers since Seb married Jillie."

Marc nodded. "I forgot that your brother is married to

Jillie Everhart. I saw that wedding on TV. Nashville really turns out for one of its own."

"It was really awesome to meet so many famous musicians." She smiled at the memory. "But you know what, Seb's wife might be a country music superstar, but she's one of the most genuine, down-to-earth women I've ever met."

"Not to mention," he finished dryly, "one of the most beautiful."

To her surprise, she felt a quick stab of jealousy. Now that was completely ridiculous. Seb and Jillie were so much in love you could feel the electricity between them from fifteen feet away. "Wait until you meet her in person. She's even more gorgeous in real life."

"What about Sebastian? He looks like a real hard-ass."

"He's been through a lot. He might appear tough, but inside he's just a big marshmallow." She had to laugh, picturing Seb's reaction if he could hear her description.

Still, in all fairness she needed to warn Marc about her overprotective older brothers.

"Dominic and Sebastian are—" she started.

"Legendary. I know," he interrupted. "I've heard stories of Seb's exploits."

"Really? From where? That's sort of surprising, since Seb was in special ops. Most of what he did was so classified his own family doesn't know about it."

Shifting in his seat, Marc gave her an uncomfortable look. "I sort of…know Dom."

This shocked her. "How?"

"When he worked for the Bureau. He and I went to Quantico at the same time."

Narrow-eyed, she studied him. "And you never mentioned this because…?"

"It really wasn't relevant. I haven't seen him since Quantico, especially since I went in a different direction." He cleared his throat. "As a matter of fact, when we spoke today it was the first time we've talked since he quit the Bureau."

Now he had her attention. "He called you today?"

"Your mother put him on the phone when I called to let her know we were running late."

"Really?" Familiar with the ways of big brothers, she crossed her arms. "What'd he have to say to you after all this time?"

"He wanted to know my intentions toward his baby sister."

She sighed. "I expected as much. What'd you say?"

His mischievous smile started the warmth blossoming inside her again. "I simply told him the truth."

And despite her best attempts, he wouldn't say any more.

As they pulled up in front of her mother's house, she barely let the car coast to a stop before she had the door open. Flashing Marc an apologetic smile, she took off running.

Halfway up the sidewalk, the front door opened and a tall, broad-shouldered man held out his arms. Watching Lea leap into them, Marc recognized Sebastian Cordasic from the tabloid photos. His rugged, austere features appeared softened by emotion as he hugged his baby sister.

Slowly, not wanting to intrude on the moment, Marc got out of his car. He took his time making his way up the sidewalk, unable to take his gaze off Lea, who practically glowed with happiness. Seeing her like this warmed his heart.

No sooner had Seb set Lea back on her feet when another man, this one with dark hair and a more athletic build, grabbed her up in a bear hug. Dominic Cordasic, Dom to his friends.

Once, he and Marc Kenyon had been good friends. There'd been a lot of water under the bridge since then.

Peering over the top of Lea's head, Dom grinned at Marc as he released his sister. Lea turned and met Marc halfway up the sidewalk, taking his arm.

"Marc Kenyon." Hand outstretched, Dom smiled warmly. "I hear you've been watching my baby sister's back."

"I don't know if I'd put it quite that way," Marc said dryly, squeezing Lea's arm. "She can take pretty good care of herself."

Sebastian waited just inside the foyer. He studied Marc with a shuttered expression while Lea made the introductions.

"Pleased to meet you," he drawled as he shook Marc's hand. "It's not every day our little sister brings a man home."

"Seb." Cheeks pink, Lea protested. "We just got done working together and—"

"Rescuing Mom and putting away the worst serial killer in recent memory is not just any case," Dom chided gently. "Take a little credit, why don't you?"

Though she shook her head, her smile told Marc she was pleased with her brother's praise.

They went inside.

"Rachel, Jillie and Mom are in the kitchen," Seb pointed out. "Though we ordered pizza, they felt like they had to whip up some fancy dessert or something."

"Come on." Tugging on Marc's arm, still linked with hers, Lea started forward eagerly. "I want you to meet Rachel and Jillie."

The doorbell rang at that moment.

"The pizza's here!" Seb and Dominic shouted in unison, jockeying to see who could open the door.

Watching all this, standing side by side with the woman he loved more deeply than ever, Marc was struck by a sense of longing so sharp, so deep, that he had to clench his teeth to keep from crying out.

This felt like…home.

The home he'd never had. The home he now knew he wanted to make with Lea, if she'd have him.

He knew they should eventually talk about this, about how they felt about each other. But he was a man of action, rather than words, and he knew he'd happily spend the rest of his life showing her how much he cared.

Judging from her actions, Lea felt the same way. He could only hope he wasn't wrong about this. If he was, then he was about to make the biggest mistake of his life.

Entering the kitchen, Marc released Lea to hug her mother, who then enveloped him also in a vanilla-scented hug. At the sink, two blonde women turned as one, and he found himself looking into two pairs of identical blue eyes, both the color of sapphires.

"Welcome!" Drying her hands on a dish towel, Jillian Everhart stepped forward and hugged him. When she released him, the other blonde, who looked so similar they had to be twins, stepped forward and held out her hand.

"Rachel Cordasic," she said. Her cool, firm grip matched her voice.

He studied her, wondering why she looked vaguely familiar, then remembering she also had been all over the news a few years back. She'd been married to a mega-rich casino owner with suspected Mafia connections who'd ended up dead.

Still cracking jokes, Dom and Seb carried the pizzas into the kitchen.

"You ordered enough to feed a small army!" Lea cried, eyeing six boxes.

"That's because Seb and Dom can each eat a large pizza by themselves," Lillian put in, smiling indulgently. "And I bet your young man can do the same."

Marc noted with some happiness that Lea did not protest her mother referring to him as *her* young man. And he could indeed put away a large pizza, along with a few cans of beer.

As if on cue, his stomach growled loudly, making them all laugh.

In a flurry of paper plates and laughter, they all dug in. Leaning back in his chair and watching, Marc couldn't help but wonder what it would have been like to grow up in a family like this.

His next thought was that if things went well, his own children would know the warmth of such a family.

They polished off every last piece of pizza, Seb and Dom sparring good-naturedly for the final slice. Stuffed, Marc took them up on their invitation to catch a football game on television in the den.

The women begged off, claiming they had to work together to cook up some sort of dessert.

As if anyone could possibly eat anything more.

In the den, Marc accepted a beer from Seb and dropped down on the couch facing the TV. If he was slightly startled when Seb took a seat on one side of him and Dom on the other, he was careful not to let this show.

"It's been a long time," Dom said, using the remote to turn on the game.

Before Marc could answer, Seb leaned over. "Why are you here with our sister?"

The direct approach. Marc could appreciate that. Still, he and Lea's relationship was nobody's business but their own. Especially since he didn't even know the status himself.

Or even if there was going to be a relationship.

Since both men were staring at him like they would jump him if he gave the wrong answer, he gave the simplest, yet still truthful reply.

"Lea and I are friends," he said firmly.

"Friends," Seb repeated, taking a long drink of his beer.

"Yes, friends." Marc raised his voice for emphasis. He glanced at Dom, to see the other man staring at something behind them.

"I sure hope for your sake that you're telling the truth," Dom said quietly. "Because that was Lea and she seemed really upset to hear you say that."

Calling herself seven kinds of fool, Lea raced down the hall, past the kitchen and into the guest bathroom, where she closed and locked the door.

Friends… Figured. Here she'd thought this relationship was a lot more. She'd never been good at judging the level of men's interest. She and Marc had had great sex, but apparently in his mind that was all it was. Great sex.

And the emotional connection? Had she simply imagined that, too?

She stood in front of the mirror, eyeing her flushed cheeks and too-bright eyes, and let her shoulders sag. The exhaustion she'd managed to hold at bay with excitement over her brothers' arrival in town came rushing back, full force.

More than anything, she needed to crash. But there were still a few things to deal with. Like—mentally, she cringed—the necessity of Marc removing his belongings from her apartment.

How would that go?

A soft tap on the door made her jump.

"Lea?" Marc. Great. Exactly who she didn't want to see right now.

"I'm kind of busy right now," she lied. "I'll be out in a few minutes."

On the other side of the door, she heard whispering. Low, masculine whispering.

"Seb? Dom? What are you two up to?"

A moment later, she had her answer. Her two buffoon brothers must have shown Marc the hidden key that Mom kept on top of the doorjamb.

The doorknob slowly turned.

"I hope you're decent," he said. "Dom assured me you would be."

"Like he knows." Suddenly, too tired to argue, she sighed.

"Come on in. What did you need?"

He came inside, locking the door behind him, then flashing her a quick grin as he placed the key on the counter. "Now no one will disturb us."

"Oh, yeah?" Crossing her arms, she rolled her eyes. "You don't know my brothers. If they want in, they'll be in here. Now, what's so important you had to find me in the bathroom to tell me?"

Instead of answering, he gathered her gently into his arms. Despite her earlier resolve, she burrowed her face into his chest and breathed his wonderful and familiar scent. He felt so big, so solidly masculine, so *right*.

*Fool.*

Pressed so tightly against her, she felt his body stir.

Friends? She felt a hot and sinful joy as her own body responded, tingling from the contact.

Heavens help her, if she didn't put a stop to this, they'd

end up making love on the floor of her mother's bathroom, with her entire family outside the door.

"Marc, I—"

"I love you." His warm breath tickled her ear.

Stunned, she froze. "You know what?" Pushing him away, she retreated to the other end of the bathroom counter. "The only thing I've ever asked from you was honesty. Now, you can't even give me that. Get out."

He didn't move. Unwittingly, she let her gaze roam over him, drinking in his masculine beauty.

"Didn't you hear me?"

A muscle worked in his strong jaw. "I did. But I'm not leaving until you hear what I've got to say."

"Save your breath." Hurt made her voice ragged, but she didn't care. She'd been through enough that day, surely she was allowed a little rawness. "I've already heard what you have to say. *Friend.* That's fine, but I don't plan on being your friend with benefits."

A small smile hovered around the edges of his mouth. "Is that why you think I'm here? To talk you into becoming my sexual plaything?"

Images of his hard, masculine body wrapped around her danced inside her head, tantalizing her. Put that way, it didn't sound half-bad.

"Why are you here?" she asked, raking her fingers through her hair. "It's been a really long day and I'm beat."

"I know you heard me telling your brothers that you were my friend. I came here because I saw you were hurt and insulted by that term and I wanted to explain to you what *friend* means to me."

Lifting her chin, she managed a tight smile. "Nice try, Kenyon. But I think I know how to define the word."

Reaching out, he stroked her arm. The mere touch of his hand sent a jolt of desire through her.

"When I marry, the woman I'll choose will be my friend. To do otherwise would be more than foolish. A friend is someone with whom I want to spend every spare moment of my time, someone I can count on, trust and… love. I love you, Lea Cordasic. And I'd like to see about making our partnership a long-term one."

Wide-eyed, she could only stare at him. When she finally found her voice, she croaked. "You mean like making our current living arrangements more permanent?"

His wide smile lit up the small room like the summer sun. "That, too," he said. "Living together is part of it, I believe."

Digging something from his pocket, he held out a small black velvet box. "I haven't had time to buy a ring, but when I was a kid, I carried this everywhere. It means a lot to me. I'd be honored if you'd wear it until we buy a real ring to replace it."

Heart skipping madly, she took the box and opened it. Nestled inside was a battered plastic decoder ring, the kind a child's hands would dig from a box of Cracker Jack.

Perfect. Completely, utterly perfect. She didn't know whether to laugh or to cry.

Throat tight, she looked from the ring to Marc, and back again. "I…"

"Take your time. You don't have to decide right this instant."

But as he said that, it all came rushing back to her. Feiney, the mess she'd been and the tall, quiet man who'd not only shown her she could be a whole woman again, but who'd always had her back.

And she knew, staring at the small plastic ring, if she accepted his proposal, he always would.

Crossing the few feet between them, she reached up and twined her fingers in his golden, California surfer-dude hair, pulling his face down for a kiss. She kissed him with a hunger that contrasted her outer veneer of calmness, kissed him with all the need and passion and love inside her soul.

"How do you know?" she asked, nuzzling his strong neck, still holding the ring box that could, if she so desired, symbolize their future together. "How do you know it's right?"

"You trust in your instincts, the same as you do when you're a cop. I've loved you for a long time, Lea Cordasic. Sometimes, when you meet someone, you just know."

*Sometimes, you just know.* Holding his solid, masculine body, breathing in his familiar scent, she reflected on the rightness of those words.

When she still didn't speak, didn't answer, he pulled back slightly and kissed the tip of her nose. "You hang on to the ring. You can give me your answer whenever you're ready."

Though his level tone sounded casual, she could see the hurt warring with love in his bright blue eyes.

Now that she'd put Feiney and that past behind her, hadn't she decided that fear would rule her life no more? What was she afraid of, other than losing him?

Sometimes, you just know.

Suddenly, joy filled her. Pushing herself up on tiptoe, she planted a quick, breathless kiss on his mouth. Then, keeping her gaze locked on his, she carefully removed the ring from its plush nest and held out her hand.

"I would love to be your lifetime friend," she said. "But I'd like you to put the ring on my finger."

With one quick motion, he did. Then, his gaze searching

hers, he pulled her closer. "Are you sure, sugar? I don't want you to have any doubts."

Pulling his face down until they were nose to nose, she looked into his blue, blue eyes and breathed his name through her parted lips. "Marc, I've never been more certain of anything in my entire life."

He crushed her to him then, his kiss savage and tender, intoxicating and possessive. They were both breathing hard when he broke away, smiling.

With a dawning sense of wonder, she saw that joy had replaced the hurt she'd seen in his gaze. "I love you," she told him.

"Not as much as I love you."

"I beg to differ."

One quick, hard kiss silenced her. "This argument could go on for the rest of our lives," he said.

"I'd like that."

Then, her hand held firmly in his, they went to tell her family the good news.

\* \* \* \* \*

# COMING NEXT MONTH

## Available October 26, 2010

ROMANTIC SUSPENSE

SRSCNM1010

# REQUEST YOUR FREE BOOKS!

## 2 FREE NOVELS PLUS 2 FREE GIFTS!

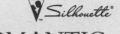

### Silhouette®

## ROMANTIC SUSPENSE

*Sparked by Danger, Fueled by Passion.*

**YES!** Please send me 2 FREE Silhouette® Romantic Suspense novels and my 2 FREE gifts (gifts are worth about $10). After receiving them, if I don't wish to receive any more books, I can return the shipping statement marked "cancel." If I don't cancel, I will receive 4 brand-new novels every month and be billed just $4.24 per book in the U.S. or $4.99 per book in Canada. That's a saving of 15% off the cover price! It's quite a bargain! Shipping and handling is just 50¢ per book.* I understand that accepting the 2 free books and gifts places me under no obligation to buy anything. I can always return a shipment and cancel at any time. Even if I never buy another book from Silhouette, the two free books and gifts are mine to keep forever.

240/340 SDN E5Q4

| Name | (PLEASE PRINT) | |
| --- | --- | --- |

| Address | | Apt. # |
| --- | --- | --- |

| City | State/Prov. | Zip/Postal Code |
| --- | --- | --- |

Signature (if under 18, a parent or guardian must sign)

### Mail to the **Silhouette Reader Service:**

**IN U.S.A.:** P.O. Box 1867, Buffalo, NY 14240-1867
**IN CANADA:** P.O. Box 609, Fort Erie, Ontario L2A 5X3

Not valid for current subscribers to Silhouette Romantic Suspense books.

**Want to try two free books from another line?**
Call 1-800-873-8635 or visit www.morefreebooks.com.

\* Terms and prices subject to change without notice. Prices do not include applicable taxes. N.Y. residents add applicable sales tax. Canadian residents will be charged applicable provincial taxes and GST. Offer not valid in Quebec. This offer is limited to one order per household. All orders subject to approval. Credit or debit balances in a customer's account(s) may be offset by any other outstanding balance owed by or to the customer. Please allow 4 to 6 weeks for delivery. Offer available while quantities last.

**Your Privacy:** Silhouette is committed to protecting your privacy. Our Privacy Policy is available online at www.eHarlequin.com or upon request from the Reader Service. From time to time we make our lists of customers available to reputable third parties who may have a product or service of interest to you. If you would prefer we not share your name and address, please check here. ☐

**Help us get it right**—We strive for accurate, respectful and relevant communications. To clarify or modify your communication preferences, visit us at www.ReaderService.com/consumerschoice.

SRS10R

# HARLEQUIN®

## A Romance

# FOR EVERY MOOD™

Spotlight on

## Inspirational

Wholesome romances
that touch the heart and soul.

See the next page
to enjoy a sneak peek from
the Love Inspired® Suspense
inspirational series.

*See below for a sneak peek from
our inspirational line, Love Inspired® Suspense*

*Enjoy this heart-stopping excerpt from
RUNNING BLIND
by top author Shirlee McCoy,
available November 2010!*

*The mission trip to Mexico was supposed to be an
adventure. But the thrill turns sour when Jenna Dougherty
and her roommate Magdalena are kidnapped.*

"It's okay. I'm here to help." The voice was as deep as the
darkness, but Jenna Dougherty didn't believe the lie. She
could do nothing but lie still as hands slid down her arms,
felt the rope around her wrists.

"I'm going to use a knife to cut you free, Jenna. Hold
still."

The cold blade of a knife pressed close to her head before
her gag fell away.

"I—" she started, but her mouth was dry, and she could
do nothing but suck in air.

"Shhh. Whatever needs to be said can be said when
we're out of here." Nick spoke quietly, his hand gentle on
her cheek. There and gone as he sliced through the ropes on
her wrists and ankles.

He pulled her upright. "Come on. We may be on
borrowed time."

"I can't leave my friend," Jenna rasped out.

"There's no one here. Just us."

"She has to be here." Jenna took a step away.

"There's no one here. Let's go before that changes."

"It's dark. Maybe if we find a light…"

"What did you say?"

"We need to turn on the light. I can't leave until I know that—"

"What can you see, Jenna?"

"Nothing."

"No shadows? No light?"

"No."

"It's broad daylight. There's light spilling in from the window I climbed in through. You can't see it?"

She went cold at his words.

"I can't see anything."

"You've got a nasty bruise on your forehead. Maybe that has something to do with it." His fingers traced the tender flesh on her forehead.

"It doesn't matter *how* it happened. I'm blind!"

*Can Nick help Jenna find her friend or will chasing this trail have Jenna running blindly again into danger?*

*Find out in RUNNING BLIND, available in November 2010 only from Love Inspired Suspense.*

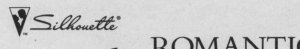

# ROMANTIC
## SUSPENSE
**Sparked by Danger, Fueled by Passion.**

# DEADLIER
*than the*
# MALE

BY *NEW YORK TIMES* AND
*USA TODAY* BESTSELLING AUTHOR

# SHARON
# SALA

**AND**

## COLLEEN THOMPSON

Women can be dangerous enemies
but love will conquer all.

*Available November wherever books are sold.*